# G R JORDAN

# The Cortado Club

*A Highlands and Islands Detective Thriller*

*First edition*

*ISBN: 978-1-914073-77-9*

*This book was professionally typeset on Reedsy.*
*Find out more at reedsy.com*

*To the wonderful team at Kopi Java, and to baristas everywhere, you are not mere servers of beverages, you are early morning superheroes!*

Given enough coffee I could rule the
world.

TERRY PRATCHETT

# Contents

# Acknowledgement

To Ken, Jessica, Jean and Rosemary for your work in bringing this novel to completion, your time and effort is deeply appreciated.

# Novels by G R Jordan

The Highlands and Islands Detective series (Crime)

1. Water's Edge
2. The Bothy
3. The Horror Weekend
4. The Small Ferry
5. Dead at Third Man
6. The Pirate Club
7. A Personal Agenda
8. A Just Punishment
9. The Numerous Deaths of Santa Claus
10. Our Gated Community
11. The Satchel
12. Culhwch Alpha
13. Fair Market Value
14. The Coach Bomber
15. The Culling at Singing Sands
16. Where Justice Fails
17. The Cortado Club
18. Cleared to Die

Kirsten Stewart Thrillers (Thriller)

1. A Shot at Democracy
2. The Hunted Child
3. The Express Wishes of Mr MacIver
4. The Nationalist Express
5. The Hunt for 'Red Anna'

The Contessa Munroe Mysteries (Cozy Mystery)

1. Corpse Reviver
2. Frostbite
3. Cobra's Fang

The Patrick Smythe Series (Crime)

1. The Disappearance of Russell Hadleigh
2. The Graves of Calgary Bay
3. The Fairy Pools Gathering

Austerley & Kirkgordon Series (Fantasy)

1. Crescendo!
2. The Darkness at Dillingham
3. Dagon's Revenge
4. Ship of Doom

Supernatural and Elder Threat Assessment Agency (SETAA) Series (Fantasy)

1. Scarlett O'Meara: Beastmaster

Island Adventures Series (Cosy Fantasy Adventure)

1. Surface Tensions

Dark Wen Series (Horror Fantasy)

1. The Blasphemous Welcome
2. The Demon's Chalice

# Chapter 1

C larissa Urquhart glanced at her watch and thought to herself, *I've got time.* Her head quickly flicked up to check the traffic in front of her as she drove the hire car to the centre of Stornoway. To her left was the inner harbour and to her right a selection of shops and hotels, above which were flats to let. One of the shops had the legend 'The Cortado Club' written above it. Clarissa had heard it mentioned as somewhere that did *proper* coffee. After an early start that morning, she decided she deserved the half an hour. Besides, it was also at the centre of the case she was about to get involved in.

Detective Inspector Macleod, Clarissa's boss, had been contacted by health authorities on the Isle of Lewis when an autopsy into potential accidental poisoning threw up some strange results. The local hospital was having difficulty trying to identify exactly what had happened. Clarissa had been brought in to look at the case from the point of view of motive and to see if the dead woman had any enemies. Macleod had deemed the case not worthy of his attention at this time, thinking that the island had got its knickers in a twist. Although from the island, he said they tended to overreact.

1

Being so insular, anything of a vaguely serious nature was suddenly blown out of all proportion.

Clarissa would normally have expected Sergeant McGrath, her direct boss, to go but Hope McGrath had declined as she had booked a weekend away with the light of her life. Clarissa smirked as she drove the car. *Car-hire man*, that's who Hope was with; *car-hire man,* known better to Hope as John. The fact he ran a car-hire facility meant the team never called him by his first name.

Clarissa reckoned this would be a routine job. After passing the Cortado Club, she saw some parking spaces on the left-hand side of the road and pulled in. On stepping out, she saw that the space was good for eight hours before she would have to move on, but she reckoned she couldn't get away with that long a break.

Wrapped up in a shawl, as was her common garb, Clarissa marched along in high boots, aware that a few people were staring over at her. She was somewhat eccentric, having come from an art background. Now into her fifties, she was not trapped by any modern styling, but simply wore what she wanted when she wanted. She said things as they were, and generally acted on her own thoughts.

Now at the later stages of her career, she was operating on the murder investigation team after spending most of her days in art-world fests. She wondered why Macleod had brought her on to the team, for often, she kicked against him. Maybe he appreciated an older head. Two other persons on the team, Hope McGrath and Alan Ross, were somewhat younger, and while immensely competent, didn't always know how to grab the bull by the horns. Clarissa could grab it by the horns and give it a kick up the backside at the same time.

2

As she arrived at the Cortado Club café, she looked in through the large windows and noticed that nearly every table was full. She marched up to the front counter. Looking up at the drink menu, she advised she would take a cortado, a double ristretto with silky milk, or at least that's what the board said. She'd never had one, quite often preferring her coffee black or with simply a drop of milk in it. When in Rome . . .

Clarissa took her seat and lay back into it, closing her eyes and taking a deep breath. Yes, this morning had been an early start. These days, they tended to hurt a lot more than when she was in her heyday. Not that she was past it by any means; never would anyone say that, or if they did, they'd get a rude awakening.

It took a few minutes before a small glass appeared in front of her, just over a thumb high. Inside was a light brown liquid and a small fluffy top with a leaf pattern embedded into it. Clarissa took hold of the cup, felt its heat, and applied her other hand to the bottom as she took a short sip. It was certainly rich in flavour. If she was to investigate this place, it certainly could have its perks.

She looked around at the staff behind the counter and saw a man she would picture as Eastern European, along with a woman she thought looked distinctly island, and a couple of other staff running here and there. The man seemed concentrated on taking cups to his coffee machine, tapping out the previous grounds and filling it again, and then watching the coffee flow. Clarissa turned back and looked out the window. It was a somewhat grey day outside, but it wasn't raining; for that, she was thankful. She glanced down on her watch. Another twenty minutes—she could afford another twenty minutes. Clarissa shut her eyes, breathed deeply, and tried to

3

take in the aroma of the small coffee in front of her.

'You're police, aren't you?'

Clarissa opened her eyes, looked to her left, and saw an elderly lady looking back at her. The woman had white hair and a skinny frame.

'What makes you say that?' asked Clarissa.

'You have a way about you.'

Clarissa thought about what the woman was saying. She didn't. Surely not. 'What do you mean?' she asked the woman.

'The way you took everything in. The way you've checked the menu. The way you're looking at what's in front of you. Now you're taking the smells of the day. I'm sure you could probably repeat the movements of everyone in here.'

*This is getting a bit crazy*, thought Clarissa. *I could probably tell you where most people were sitting*, she thought to herself, *but I'm not going to let that out.*

'What if I am police?'

'Well, you know what happened here. She died, didn't she? She died. I'd have thought that they'd have sent somebody else over though. After all, you don't seem that interested.'

'Interested?' said Clarissa. 'I'm currently sitting and having a coffee. Who says I'm working whatever case you're on about?'

Clarissa could see that there was some interest in her, and several other people had started to move over in her direction. 'Here,' said the old woman. 'Boris, police are here.'

'Excuse me,' said Clarissa, 'you don't need to make a sideshow of this.'

'So, you're not here to investigate. Is that what you're telling me?' said the old woman.

A man emerged from behind Clarissa, and she recognised him as the man making the coffee.

'Are you here to question me?' asked the man in an Eastern European accent.

Clarissa was stuck. She couldn't answer no because, actually, that probably was going to happen. On the other hand, she didn't want to say yes either, because everyone would have their backs up, suddenly frightened of this person who had just snuck in.

'It has nothing to do with the coffee. My coffee is the finest. I make it myself or my wife makes it. There are only two hands on the coffee, never anyone else.'

'Well, it certainly is nice coffee,' said Clarissa, as she started to feel a little flustered, 'but now is not the time for this. I may be back to talk to you later.'

'Why later?'

'Because I'm having my break,' said Clarissa. 'I came in to sit down and have a break. I only just came over from the mainland this morning.'

'Yet you came straight in here?' queried the old woman.

'Yes, that sounds a bit strange,' said someone behind her.

'Look, I'm not taking this,' said Clarissa. 'I really am not taking this. Everyone just go back to what you were doing. I'm just going to sit here, I'm going to finish my coffee, and then I'm going to leave. Currently, I'm not on duty; I'm having my break.'

'You people are never on break,' said the old woman. 'Trust me, Boris, they're never on break.'

'Who might you be?' asked Clarissa.

'One of Boris's customers, just a little bit more observant than everybody else,' she said.

'That's not answering my question,' said Clarissa.

'You said you weren't on duty,' said an angry Boris, and

5

his wife appeared beside him. Boris was slightly smaller than Clarissa, but he seemed extremely agitated. He had a moustache that may have been trimmed down from bushier days and hair that was starting to fade at the back. His wife, on the other hand, was a tall brunette. Clarissa thought she had those island eyes, ones that could switch from extremely welcoming to penetrating in an instant.

'Is she here, Boris, to see us? What is she doing here?'

'I have just told your husband,' said Clarissa, putting her hand up, 'that I am on my break. I have come in for a coffee, and very good coffee it is, too. When I have finished it, I will leave. Now, if everyone would just sit down and mind your own business.'

It was the first hint of agitation in Clarissa's voice, and she knew it shouldn't have come out.

'What do you expect?' said someone behind the old woman. 'You come in here unannounced. That's not how you do it, is it?'

*No, it wasn't how we do it*, thought Clarissa, *but I was only coming in for a coffee. I was nobody. It's not uncommon to scout the ground beforehand. Even if I was scouting, all I wanted was a coffee.*

Clarissa stood up and her chair scraped. She pushed it back along the floor, 'Everyone sit down, okay? Just sit down.'

The action may have been meant to calm everyone, but all it did was raise more agitation. Several other customers had now come in looking for take-out coffee, and were standing in a queue closely behind Boris.

'Boris, what's the hold up here, mate?'

'This detective is the hold up. She's come in, and she's sitting in our place.'

'I'm not holding you up at all,' said Clarissa. 'Just go back to making these people coffee.'

'Boris, I haven't got long. Two minutes I need to be out of here. Can I get a flat white?'

'Of course, I'll get you a flat white in a minute. I need to talk to this woman.'

'You do not need to talk to me,' said Clarissa. Her face was now going red, and she could feel the anger building up inside. 'Please, Boris, 'she said, 'just go behind the serving bar and start doing coffees for everyone. If I need to, I will talk to you later.'

'What did they say to you? What did the public health people say to you? Did they tell you that I poisoned him? I never poisoned him.'

The coffee house had only been mentioned as a possible place where the poison could have been ingested. There was a number of other places, and that was why Clarissa felt it was okay to come and enjoy a coffee. Besides, how do you poison somebody with a coffee? What was in a coffee that can actually kill someone? It wasn't like if you were serving a chicken salad and you could get caught out with salmonella.

'Look, Boris, I really need to go. Can you just get me—'

Clarissa saw Boris turn round. 'Shut up. Just shut up. Do you know how important this is to me? Do you know how serious this is? They're here, here trying to investigate.'

Boris's wife put her hands on his shoulders. 'Easy, easy, love. Now, you don't want to be saying that to customers. We don't want to be—'

'Poisoning? So, what, they reckon it came from here?' said another woman, completely out of the blue.

Clarissa put her hands up. 'Stop. Just stop.'

But no one did, and the din continued to rise. Fingers

7

were now wagging; comments were being made. One person stormed out of the shop. Clarissa saw on the far corner by a sofa at the window, one man didn't flinch. She wondered why and looked at him. He was an older gentleman, maybe in his sixties. At first, she thought he was asleep, but the chest didn't rise. She pushed her chair back further, stepped aside from the table, only to have several people move closer to her, firing questions at her.

'Aside. Get out of my way,' she said, almost angrily. But inside, she was concerned for the man. A woman moved to one side, but a short man stepped in front of her.

'You need to tell Boris why you're here. There's no point coming in here . . .'

The man was swept aside with a hand as Clarissa increased her pace towards the far table. As she arrived at the sofa, she sat down beside the man and put two hands up to his neck. She then moved her hands down to his wrist.

'Ambulance,' said Clarissa, turning around to Boris. 'Get an ambulance now. He's not breathing.' She continued to look for a pulse but found none. She reached up, tilted his head back and began to blow into his mouth. She then reached down, turned his legs round so he was laying on the sofa. Her first aid training, which had been locked in her brain by the extensive course some years ago, was trying to escape. She tried to remember how to do it, how to press down, when there was a tap at her shoulder.

'Excuse me, love. I'm a nurse. I'll do this. Do it with me.'

Together they worked on the man, Clarissa following the instructions, breathing air into the man when necessary, through his mouth. She could feel the tension around her. Then when the blue lights arrived outside the shop, she stepped aside as two paramedics took over the efforts to resuscitate the man. She stood for five minutes watching them, before they too stepped back. One of them took a blanket from out of the ambulance and covered the man up.

'So, he's dead?' asked Clarissa.

'Yes,' said the paramedic. 'What happened to him?'

'I don't know,' said Clarissa. 'I was over at the table there; all hell was breaking loose in here. I looked over, but he didn't seem to be breathing, so I just started to work on him. I got joined by the nurse.'

'Well, there doesn't seem to be much life about him. We'll have to see what they say back at the hospital, but as far as I can gather, I'm not sure there's much you could have done.'

Clarissa turned away feeling that was cold comfort. 'I'll tell them anyway,' she said. 'I'm up there soon.' Then Clarissa looked around to see the onlookers watching closely.

'It was not my coffee,' said Boris. Clarissa realised how the scene must have looked. *Macleod's going to be livid*, she thought, *absolutely livid*.

# Chapter 2

Clarissa lurked in a small breakout area in the Western Isles Hospital, awaiting a doctor to come and fetch her. The dead man had been taken into the hospital and removed down to the morgue. Clarissa had managed to follow the ambulance up to the hospital. She wanted to speak directly to those who had worked on the first body, which had apparently been food poisoning, and see what they made of the second body, hoping they would be able to make some sort of connection if one was there.

She was also pacing up and down because, at some point, she'd have to explain what happened to Macleod, and he wasn't going to see it as the most professional behaviour. A smart man, possibly in his thirties, attended Clarissa, dressed in a bright blue shirt and black trousers. In some ways, she thought he looked like a doctor off the television, one of those perfect people, and he smiled as he approached.

'You must be Detective Sergeant Clarissa Urquhart,' said the man. 'Did I get that correct?'

'You most certainly did,' said Clarissa. 'And who are you?'

'Dr John Constance, and I think you should come with me because you may find some interest in what I have to say.'

'Oh, by all means,' said Clarissa. 'Lead the way.'

The man took Clarissa down several corridors before turning into a small office. Inside, Clarissa could see papers piled high on shelves, medical books here and there, and records sitting about. There was a filing cabinet, one chair beside a large computer, and a small brown-covered chair that John Constance pulled out for Clarissa to sit on.

'My apologies. It's not exactly the biggest of offices,' he said, sitting down, his knees almost touching Clarissa's.

'It's perfectly fine,' she said. 'What can you tell me?'

'Well, as you know, we suspected food poisoning on the first death of Miranda Folly. It appears to be poisoning, looking at what happened to her system and how it shut down. She seems to have ingested something that stopped the system, but we can't find exactly what. That being said, we're not exactly a forensic unit, which is why we requested your help. We're looking to try and trace back and see if the food substance came from any particular local vendor. There's also the possibility that she took something at home incorrectly. But, as you know, she was at some point inside the Cortado Club, and that's why we listed it as one of our potential places where the poisoning took place. Donald MacDonald . . .'

'Sorry,' said Clarissa. 'Donald MacDonald?'

'Yes,' said John. 'I know, but it's pretty common here on the island. He was known as Donny Tubes apparently.'

'Tubes? Why was he known as Tubes?'

'Apparently, it was from the past from what he liked when he was a young boy, penne pasta, except they all called it tubes. So, he got the name Donny Tubes, but Donald MacDonald—Donny Tubes—seems to have had a shutdown of the body in exactly the same way. Now we suspect that it was possibly food-based, but we are looking beyond that. Like I say, I think we could do with a little assistance.'

'I didn't think you could poison somebody with coffee. It'd be quite hard.'

'If it wasn't an extraneous matter put into the coffee, yes, it would be. The milk could be off, but you'd taste it. Coffee itself is freshly made. If you were grinding it up and it was off, you'd see it. You would have some sort of mould or something else. It's very hard to food poison someone with such a liquid substance. That's why we thought you should come and take a look at it.'

'Well, to be honest, the boss wasn't that keen. That's why I'm over here, but we've got two deaths in our hands now, potential for coincidence, but that would seem unlikely.'

'That's what I thought,' said the doctor, 'but like I say, we'll accept any assistance you can give us.'

'Well, thank you very much for your time,' said Clarissa. 'Continue to have a look, but I suspect our forensic team will be over shortly and liaise with you directly. You can talk to them in better jargon than you can with me.'

The doctor shook her hand. 'It's been a pleasure,' he said. 'And here's my number in case you need to contact me.' The man handed over a small card, which Clarissa pocketed before passing one of her own back to him.

'I must go and see the local station, find out what they make of it,' said Clarissa, 'but thank you for your help, doctor.' The man escorted her right to the front of the building where Clarissa picked up her mobile phone, placing a call back to Inverness. Once she got the switchboard, she asked for Macleod and nervously tapped her foot, waiting for him to respond.

'This is Macleod.'

'Seoras, it's Clarissa. There's another one dead here.'

'What? I only sent you over this morning and you've got two down already.'

'Don't take that tone with me. I had to try and give him the kiss of life.'

'Are you okay?' asked Macleod, his voice suddenly changing.

'Yes, I'm fine,' she said.

'But you want to give me a rundown of how it happened?'

'Well, I went into the coffee shop, the one that was a possible point of suspicion. And when I was in there, a man collapsed and I tried to provide first aid, but we lost him. The hospital's saying it looks like the same sort of thing.'

'I'm sorry,' said Macleod. 'So, you were in questioning the staff?'

'No, Seoras. I wasn't.' Clarissa waited for the next bit.

'So why were you in?'

'I stopped in for five minutes before I was heading up to the hospital.'

'Okay,' said Macleod. 'So, what, you were just sitting there when this happened?'

Clarissa knew she would have to come clean. If she didn't, Macleod could walk into a storm when he first arrived and have no idea what anybody was on about.

'I went in and sat down for ten minutes to try and get my head together before I went up to the hospital. But when I was there, an old woman asked if I was a policewoman.'

'And you said what?'

'Well, we can't lie, can I? Eventually, I said, yes. She then kicked off about whether or not I was investigating the owner. The owner got involved. To be fair, there was quite a ruckus.

And then I had to fight my way through to try and save this poor bloke.'

'You only left this morning,' said Macleod. 'It was just a routine poisoning, possible food poisoning case. How am I getting this? Is this going to be on the news?'

'I don't think it's important enough to be on the news,' said Clarissa. 'Might make a few of the local papers. The phone went silent. Clarissa stood, tapping her foot, waiting for the response.

'Two dead. Coincidence?'

'To be honest, Seoras, I don't know. The hospital over here is having trouble just working out exactly what the poisoning element is. They could probably do with help from forensic.'

'What's your gut saying?' asked Macleod.

'I think they're linked,' said Clarissa. 'The doctor said they both died in very similar fashion and how unlucky to get food poisoning twice. How do you get food poisoning in a coffee shop, Seoras? Sure, it's got to be one of the safest things you can do. Drink coffee.' Again, the phone went silent. 'Seoras, are you there? Look, I know it's not good but are you—?'

'Get down to the coffee shop again. Make sure they gather up all the evidence. See what he was drinking. Make sure to clock who was there and take over the investigation. I'll be over by tonight at the latest.'

'Of course, Seoras. I'll get onto it now.'

'But, Urquhart,' said Macleod, using her second name.

'Yes, boss?'

'I don't expect to see you sitting having coffee when I arrive.'

'No, boss, I'm on it.' With that, Clarissa closed down the call. Making her way back to her car, Clarissa drove it back into Stornoway and parked up again outside the coffee house.

The front door was closed, and she could see a number of police cars around it. Inside were a number of uniforms. As she approached the door, an officer questioned what she was doing. The man had obviously arrived later than the rest, but she showed her credentials to him and then entered.

'Excuse me,' she announced as she walked in, 'I'm looking for the officer in charge.'

A blonde-haired woman approached, her hair tied up behind her. 'I'm Sergeant Dolan and I take it you're the officer involved in this incident.'

'That's correct. I'm Detective Sergeant Clarissa Urquhart.' Clarissa handed over her credentials for the woman to see. 'I have to tell you that my boss, Detective Inspector Macleod, will be making his way over. At this time, we are taking over the investigation. Can I ask what you've done so far?'

'By all means. We've tried to interview everyone who was here. We still have to interview yourself, but you can obviously make a statement on that.'

'What about the evidence?'

'What evidence?' asked Sergeant Dolan.

'The man was poisoned or at least we suspect so.'

'Right,' said Dolan, looking around at the table behind her. 'He was sat over there, wasn't he?'

'That's correct.'

Dolan started to redden in the face then walked over to the counter. 'Excuse me, Boris,' she said, looking at the owner. 'Did anybody touch the cup that was on that table?'

'I didn't,' he said.

'Did anybody take Mr. MacDonald's cup?' asked Sergeant Dolan aloud looking around. 'Did anybody take it away?'

'I was first on the scene,' said a police constable. 'And there

15

was no cup there.' Clarissa made her way over to him.

'Look, are you sure?' asked Clarissa. 'This is very important.'

'I came in and you were just going out, off up to the hospital. I remember you said to me that the man had died, so I came in, started taking statements, talking to everyone, made sure I got the names of who was here. The rest of the officers joined, but I never saw any cup.'

Clarissa sat down, closed her eyes, and tried to think back to the incident. She had been sitting down. There'd been a lot of noise and suddenly, she stood up and turned back to Boris. 'Boris, did you serve him coffee?'

'Yes, I did.'

'What was it?' asked Clarissa.

'Cortado. He always had a cortado.'

'It would've been served in one of those little glasses like you served me.'

'Yes, that's a cortado, that's what it comes in. That's how you make a cortado. Double ristretto, milk on top, silky, foam. Yes, that's cortado.'

'Did he have anything with it?'

'No, Donald MacDonald never had anything with it. Tubes just had cortado. People he came in with, they have cake, they have this and that—Tubes, just cortado.' Clarissa realised Boris's English was good but not his first language.

'How long had he been in here for?' asked Clarissa.

'Maybe an hour. He always came in and sat and looked out. That's what he did.'

'He spent an hour drinking that thing? It's tiny,' said Clarissa. 'I couldn't make a normal cup of coffee last that long.'

'He always did,' said Boris. 'Sometimes wondered why he was here.'

'Was anybody with him?' asked Clarissa.

'Not that I saw—unusual because quite often, he does have people with him.'

'Okay. We'll get into that later. As of now, we're going to have to close your cafe, Boris. You're not going to be opening tomorrow. This is a crime scene.'

'How is it a crime scene? I serve coffee. I serve coffee, I serve cake. Man collapses and dies; it's not my fault.'

'Two people have died.'

'Miranda, she did not die here. She died in her house.'

'But they suspect she died from food poisoning. This is somewhere she visited, Boris. Donald was here.'

'But you can't "food poison" somebody with coffee. The milk, it came today from the shop up the road. The coffee is just coffee. There is water. The water is from tap into machine. It goes into the machine, the machine boils it. We make the coffee. We make the ristretto, slow extraction. It comes out. We put the milk in, the milk is steamed. It goes from cold to steamed. There is nothing to poison people,' said Boris, becoming extremely agitated.

'Calm down,' said Clarissa. 'Just calm down. Nobody said you poisoned them. We just have to look at all angles.'

'But if he didn't poison them,' said the police constable who was first on the scene, 'And the man was poisoned here, then you're suggesting that—'

'Someone did it,' said Clarissa. 'Somebody actively put poison in.'

'So, it's not food poison we're looking at,' said Sergeant Dolan.

Clarissa took Sergeant Dolan to one side and whispered, 'Yes, we could be looking at murder. That's why DI Macleod is on his way, and I suspect in his head, he thinks it is too. He doesn't come this far for no reason.'

'Then I'll make sure we get our statements done. That's important,' said Dolan, 'that the cup is missing.'

'Yes, it is but who was here over the last hour of Donald MacDonald's life, that becomes very important.'

'I'll get onto it then,' said Dolan. 'Try and get you a picture.'

'Good,' said Clarissa. 'If you can get it done before Macleod arrives, all the better.'

# Chapter 3

Seoras Macleod stepped from the airport building, looking for a car and saw a purple-haired detective sergeant waiting for him. Next to her was Hope McGrath, his travelling companion and red-headed, six-feet-tall detective sergeant, who ran his unit for him. Seeing the pair of them, he should have had a sense of comfort, but Macleod always felt strange about coming back to the island. This was his home, where he had come from, where he had lost his wife, a suicide at Holm point.

Over the years, he had struggled to change the religious bent that had been bred into him, one where souls were seen with a different set of eyes. Whilst he still remembered the good parts of it, the solid upbringing, the truth about what was right and wrong, he also saw the controlling side of it. A side that never wanted people to flourish for themselves. One that struggled to see beauty in the bleaker weather. Especially on the few days when the sun shone, he always felt as if something toxic had stayed with him.

Things had changed. Of course, they had, but to Seoras, there was always a black blot of those deadly values that may have cost his wife's life.

'Jane is looking for an explanation why I'm here,' Macleod said to Clarissa Urquhart. Jane was his partner and had settled down with Macleod on the edge of Inverness. From Cornwall, she had no hang-ups like Macleod did with the island. He had found her to be such a refreshing change in the days when he was struggling. She kept him fresh and lively. The first thing she had said to him on hearing he was departing for the island again was a simple, 'Why? Can't Clarissa handle it?'

'You're here, sir, because you decided to come.'

'She asked me, "Couldn't Clarissa handle it?"' said Macleod. 'Do you know what I told her?'

'Do I want to know?' asked Clarissa.

'No,' said Macleod. 'Where's the car?'

Clarissa pointed over to her car sitting in the car park. Macleod walked past her, pulling a small case behind him and Hope McGrath turned to Clarissa, smiling broadly.

'He said, "She picked a fight in a coffee shop."'

'He never.'

'Oh yes,' said Hope. 'Tells Jane everything; never forget that.'

Hope grinned as she walked off behind Macleod and Clarissa shook her head knowing it was going to take some time to live this one down.

As they sat in the car, Clarissa, once more, ran through the events of the day, explaining the exact order of how things had happened. She also had tried to recall who else had been in the building and said that together with the statements made by the Stornoway police force, she was building up a picture of people who could have been involved.

'We don't know it was done from inside the shop, do we? In fact, we still don't know what the suspected poison is.'

'No,' said Clarissa, 'but my hunch is it came from in there.

Twice this has happened. Sure, the other woman was at home, but our second victim was lying in that coffee shop. It would be incredible timing if they poisoned him elsewhere.'

'We're still clutching at straws, though,' said Macleod. 'I agree with you, Clarissa, I really do. I have the feeling it's about the coffee shop too but without Jona confirming, let's not get too excited.'

Clarissa nodded and Macleod explained that he wanted to go first to the station just to get his bearings and also to drop off his bags.

'I've put you into a hotel at the top of town if that's all right, sir?' asked Clarissa.

*She's using sir*, thought Macleod. *It must have been bad.* He gave a nod and sat back with his own thoughts as the car continued through Stornoway to the police station. Once they had parked up, the trio went inside and upstairs to a room set aside for them.

'Ross will be along presently,' said Macleod. 'He was wanting to be there when they got some of the gear off the plane. When he gets here let him run the room, Clarissa. I need you to be at the crime scene working amongst people. Ross is perfectly capable of handling the troops here. He's met them before, and he works well with them. Nice, engaging man after all. Can handle the public too,' said Macleod with a wry smile. Once again, Clarissa just shook her head.

'Good evening, Detective Inspector,' said a female voice and Macleod turned around to see a police sergeant standing at the other end of the room. 'I hope we can make you comfortable here. Whatever you need, just advise us. I'm Sergeant Dolan.'

'Thank you, Sergeant. How's it been in the interim before I came over?'

21

'Things are getting a little bit heated, Inspector. The owners of the café, Boris Yentov and his wife, Alison Smith, have been in a tizzy. There's been a lot of people passing by the shop and some not saying very nice things.'

'Foreigner,' said Macleod. 'He's the one targeted. They want to think it's anybody not from the island.'

'Hardly think that's fair, Inspector,' said Sergeant Dolan.

'How long have you been here, Sergeant?'

'Six months, Inspector.'

'Give it time; you'll learn but what else has happened?'

'The deceased man's family, I went to see them to explain what had happened. They've not taken it well. Some of them made threats towards the shop owners. I've got my people down at the shop with the owners. They're not wishing to close up for fear that somebody's going to do something to their shop. It's a pity they've only been going three years and seem to have made a great success of it. "Best coffee in town," they say.'

'Oh, I could vouch for that,' said Clarissa and then sat down again, hiding her face from Macleod.

'I'm sure you can,' said Macleod. 'I should go down and taste some of this coffee. I think we should also speak to this couple as soon as—what's the name of the deceased man again?'

'Donald MacDonald,' said Sergeant Dolan.

'MacDonald doesn't really give a lot away. What sort of family?'

'Large family, sir, known by a lot of people around here. Quite well thought of. There's quite a lot of anger going about because of it.'

'We haven't declared anything about the death yet. We haven't claimed this as murder, not gone on the record?'

'Of course not. "Inquiries are continuing;" that's all I've said.'

'Good work, Dolan. We'll go down and see that couple then we'll try and get them away from the building. The last thing we need is a focal point for the community to go out to. Detective Constable Ross will be here shortly. When he comes, give him every assistance. He'll set up an incident room and you are to take instruction from him, Sergeant, if that's okay?'

'If that's what you wish, sir. You have our resources as best as we have them available. As you probably know, we're not a massive unit here in the island.'

'I'm well aware of the island, and I'm well aware of all your restrictions, Sergeant Dolan. I thank you for your assistance so far. This may be a case of misunderstanding, or it may be a coincidence that we have two deaths from food poisoning. However, my gut instinct is there's something more behind this. That's why I'm here. Our forensic lead, Jona Nakamura, will be dropping by as well. She'll need a room and she'll also be working closely with the hospital, up at the morgue to try and identify what killed our victims.'

'You said victims, sir,' said Sergeant Dolan.

'I did. Slip of the tongue. That's why I don't like talking to the press but I do believe they will be victims.'

'Yes, sir.'

'And one more thing,' said Hope McGrath. 'Sergeant Dolan, the inspector's quite fond of his coffee so if we can have some sort of filter coffee set up in here.' Macleod glanced over at Hope, giving her a rather agitated look.

'What?' said Hope. 'Said as it is.'

'Come on,' said Macleod, 'let's go see this couple.'

The Cortado Club was only a short distance from the police station. Macleod decided to walk round and Hope watched him suck in deep breaths of air as soon as he was outside. She looked strangely at him.

'The familiar old smells,' he said. 'You get that, Clarissa, don't you?' He turned to look over his shoulder at his older sergeant, but she seemed rather sheepish, keeping her distance from him. 'Now, now,' he said. 'No need to be like that. You dropped one, Clarissa. Where's that fighting spirit? I expect you to kick back harder than that.'

'Yes, Inspector, will do.'

Macleod marched on down the street towards the harbour area of Stornoway and on arrival, he saw a small crowd chanting and shouting abuse through the doors of the coffee shop. As he got closer one of them turned to him recognising him almost instantly.

'Macleod, you here to sort this out?'

Macleod looked at the man, 'I am here to investigate and find out what's going on. If you'll kindly go home and let me get on with my job.'

'Look Macleod, it's pretty obvious what's happened.'

Clarissa stepped in front of Macleod. 'The inspector said, "Would you go home?" He was making a request. If you don't, I'll make it one of two options, the other being a night in the cells.'

Macleod marched past Clarissa entering the shop and he could hear Hope breathing hard behind him. He turned to look at the sergeant. 'A bit heavy-handed. It's good to see she's back up and at it though.' He turned round to one of the constables in the shop. 'Detective Inspector Macleod; where are the owners?'

'The seat in the corner,' said the man. 'He hasn't been off the phone. Seems to be talking to the bank or brothers or something. Something about money.'

'Well, I'm going to speak to him now. Let's give him something to do.' Hope tapped Macleod on the shoulder. 'I appreciate seeing what you're doing, sir, but I think we might want to put something up in front of that window. The people are still out there.'

Macleod turned and shouted to the door, 'Urquhart, why are those people still there?'

Macleod turned away and walked over to a man and woman sitting on a sofa. 'Good evening; my name's Detective Inspector Seoras Macleod. This is Detective Sergeant Hope McGrath, and we're here to find out what's been going on. I take it you are Boris Yentov and Alison Smith.'

'Yes, that's right. I am Boris; this is Alison, but we didn't do anything.'

'We're going to have a little chat, sir, about what happened and what has been happening, but I hear you're quite good with the coffee. Cortado, is it?'

'That's the name on the door, sir.'

'Well,' said Macleod, 'let's have one. McGrath will take one and if I don't get Urquhart one, she'll complain. Any other officers in here want one?' Macleod looked around but the three police officers shook their heads.

'The boys there are worried,' said Macleod to the young couple. 'Worried that if they drink in here, they'll be tainted as if they're on your side. I'm not on your side. I just like my coffee, but I am here for the truth and not what everybody thinks so please sir, put your phone down, get me my Cortado, then we'll have a chat.'

Macleod sat down in the sofa opposite, joined by Hope, and smiled at the woman. He noted her long brunette hair and how she tried to slide it across her face but the tears welling up in her eyes were all too obvious. It was a few minutes before the man returned, placing a Cortado in front of Macleod, one in front of McGrath, and another on the table.

'For the other woman, you said.'

'Detective Sergeant Urquhart.' Macleod turned around, looked out the window, able to see the street beyond cars passing by and no one peering in.

'Officers,' said Macleod to the Stornoway force that were in the room. 'It'd be appreciated if you all go and stand outside. Make sure we have no peeping toms.'

The men nodded and made their way out. Clarissa entered, pulling a seat up close to the couple.

'Now then,' said Macleod, 'someone said you made a go of this place. Is that correct?'

'Made a go of?' asked Boris. 'What do you mean?'

'Boris, he's paying us a compliment. We started up and the first three years have been good. We have lots of customers, that's correct, Inspector, but you don't make a business in three years. We need to keep going. Keep going to pay the bills, keep the roof over our heads. Today is a disaster.'

'Is that why you were on the phone?' Macleod asked the man. 'Were you trying to get some sort of backup?'

'We can't afford to close,' said Boris. 'We can't allow for shop to lose trade for weeks. The people outside—they're shouting at us, telling us to shut up shop. I can't do that. This is my life. This is our livelihood. We came here to make a business. I found Alison on holiday in Bulgaria and I came back with her. Her family, they welcomed me. Everything is good and now this. For something I didn't do. Why do they accuse me?'

'Has it been happening for a while?'

'When Miranda Folly died, Inspector,' said Alison, 'that's when it started, the accusations. The health people got involved. They came and they checked us like they checked everybody else, but we were targeted by other people saying that we'd done it.'

'Who exactly?'

'It was many different people, Inspector. I couldn't narrow it down to one and then rumour builds on rumour; you know how it is. Now today, look, Donald died. Donald was one of our best customers. Why would we have killed off Donald? He has a massive family. This is a disaster for us. We would have no reason to kill our people. Miranda too. She was consistent. She was here every day like Donald. They all came for the coffee. The last thing we need to do is kill them off.'

'Did you know who was in here today, during the time Donald was here?'

'I find it difficult to say,' said Boris. 'We have the takeout as well. I was just busy making the coffees. The girls who go out and serve, bring the cups back, they have a better idea.'

'I'm similar,' he said to Alison. 'I've told other officers who I thought I saw, roughly when I thought they were here. I believe they're trying to find, check out through for you.'

McGrath looked over Urquhart, and she nodded. 'Should have that shortly, sir; certainly, before the nights out.'

'Good,' said Macleod. 'That might help us. Look, at the moment, we don't know what happened. The forensic officer's coming over, and we will find out how these people died. In the meantime, I would suggest a short closure.'

'I can't close,' said Boris. 'We need to keep open. We have done nothing wrong.'

'No, you haven't. But at the moment by staying open, you're

creating a crowd and a scene. You need to understand that Donald MacDonald's family are hurting, and they are looking for someone to blame. Someone is pointing them in your direction, and they will come, and we will have more fracas. I'm not saying you have to close for a long time, maybe just a day or two until we get on top of this, then you open again with a clear name. I think I'm making sense.'

As the words left Macleod's mouth, he heard the crash behind him. He turned around and saw the window smashed, the glass lying across the floor beside a large rock with a piece of paper written around it. Hope jumped off the sofa, ran outside shouting at the officers, did they have a number plate? Macleod stood up, edged over carefully amongst the broken glass and with a handkerchief over his hand, picked up the rock that had come in. Once he lifted it onto the table, he put on some gloves and pulled out the note that was strapped around the rock, opened it, and read it back to the couple behind him. *Go home, murderers* were the only words on the paper.

# Chapter 4

The day had turned to night, and Hope McGrath was sitting beside Sergeant Dolan as her colleague drove a police car out to the edge of Stornoway. After the rock had been thrown into the Cortado Club, smashing the window, Macleod had ordered the entire front facia boarded up, and constables were posted outside for the night. Clarissa Urquhart had taken the couple home and was going to sit with them through the night in case they came up with anything different. Macleod was also aware of how stretched the Stornoway force was, and by providing an extra person to look after the cafe owners whom he saw as victims, he felt he was contributing towards Sergeant Dolan's manning difficulties.

Macleod had dispatched Hope to look into Miranda Folly's life. He had read the reports of how she had been in the coffee house the day she died, but how she'd also visited other shops. The health authority had noted where she'd bought her meat, what supermarket she'd shopped at, and such like and he had a feeling about the woman from it, but he didn't know her. So, he had sent Hope to build up a better picture of the deceased woman.

As Macleod had said to her, the police originally, and

the health authority, were looking for a connection to an accidental food poisoning. Macleod more and more felt there could be a deadlier connection, and if it was murder they were looking at, they needed to build up an image of the people who had died.

The house was situated on the outskirts of Stornoway. As they pulled up into the driveway, Hope looked both ways, but was struggling to see any other houses. The house sat in a little dale and was shaded from the remainder of the day's light. Hope thought it still looked quite quaint as the car headlights flashed over it.

It was a small cottage, possibly two rooms upstairs and she thought she could see a kitchen at the rear. Sergeant Dolan had brought the keys. As they walked along the stone path, a crunch under their feet, the sergeant led the way up to the front door and opened it. Once inside, she flicked the switch and put on the hall lights.

Hope entered and noticed the floral wallpaper going up the stairs. There was a worn carpet underneath and she saw several pairs of boots, some knee-length, some ankle, but there were no trainers. On the wall hung several coats and Hope was taken by how stylish the woman was. Yet, there was a myriad of colours. Clearly, she had a bright sense of what to wear and she couldn't find anything that was dull.

Beside the front door was a full-length mirror and Hope could imagine Miranda Folly staring at herself before she departed. There was nothing untoward in that; some people just liked to know they looked all right before they went out, but the full-length mirror bothered her. Maybe that was just a little over-the-top.

'In her forties, wasn't she?' asked Hope.

'Forty-one,' said Sergeant Dolan. 'Quite a snappy dresser if I remember right. Used to see her about town. Didn't have a car though—always got the bus. Didn't believe in cars. Didn't believe in a lot of things.'

'All right,' said Hope. 'An environmental person.'

'In some ways. Also, liked a little bit of privacy. I'm not sure many people ever came out here.'

'What about her shopping habits?' asked Hope. 'I heard that you looked into that.'

'Well, she was like all of us at the supermarket a lot of the time, but very into the delis, high-class, quality food.'

Hope opened the door into a sitting room and saw where a fire would've been lit. It was an open fire, unusual these days for the island, where most people would've had a stove, but Hope could see the remnants and smell the wood that would've burnt in there. Either side of the fireplace were two dog sculptures, long and elegant dachshunds. There seemed to be a myriad of lights as well in the room and hanging from the ceiling was what looked like wind chimes. She saw on the table a number of books. Making her way over, Hope started to pick through them. They were romance novels but Hope thought they were on the stronger side. Certainly not the sort of thing a good churchwoman would read. She thought Macleod might even be shocked by them.

'They found her in bed, I hear.'

'Yes,' said Dolan. 'She was upstairs in bed, not wearing a stitch, but that was not unusual for her, from what we've heard. That's why she liked to live remote. Was one with nature, you could say.'

'I don't mind a bit of nature,' said Hope. 'I don't have to walk around stalkers in it though.' She smiled over at Dolan, who

31

laughed.

'No. What I mean is it wasn't unusual for her to sleep that way, there was no nightwear upstairs.'

'When did you find her?'

'Well, it was funny; it was the postman who came in. In the morning, he had a parcel and the place being what it is, and we don't lock our doors, he knocked on the door and he shouted, couldn't get anybody in, but he saw her handbag was still in the hallway. That was key to knowing she was in, so he thought there was something wrong. He shouted several times. Then, he searched the place because she was never out that early in the morning.'

'What, he just found her in bed with nothing on?'

'Yes, asleep, he thought at first. She wasn't awake so he shouted from the door having closed it because he didn't want to give her a fright and then got closer, to find out she was dead. She died in the night.'

'Well, as best can be told by the post-mortem, yes, but what made people suspicious?' asked Hope.

'When they did the post-mortem, they felt that the body had been poisoned in some way. They were struggling to find out what, so then communicated with the health officials. They started investigating. They just couldn't trace exactly what it was.'

Hope wandered out into the kitchen. As she went through the cupboards, she noticed a couple of quite strange-looking egg cups.

'That's a bit of a funny one,' said Hope.

Dolan laughed, 'If my husband came home with something like that,' she said, 'I'd hit him.' One of the egg cups had a man's penis sticking out of the front of it. While two others resembled a pair of boobs.

'It's like a cheeky night at Blackpool, isn't it?' said Hope. She worked her way through the rest of the crockery in the kitchen. There was a set of plates with quite an erotic bent to them, and Hope began to feel that she was getting a picture of the woman. 'She's quite sexually orientated, isn't she?' said Hope, reaching down to pull some flyers out of a magazine rack. She held them up to Dolan. 'Did she ever go to these events?'

'I don't know,' said Dolan, looking at the advertisement for some erotic conventions. 'She probably would have kept it quite quiet here; word goes around on the island.' Hope nodded, opened up the fridge, and found some smelly cheese inside.

'Is anybody coming to clear this place up?' asked Hope.

'Well, she's not been dead that long, and we can't find a next of kin; that's the problem. We're just waiting to see if anything comes up on that. If it does, it'll be their issue. If not, well, we'll get the cleaners round, gut the place out, once we know it's going to the state, and not to anybody else.'

Hope returned to the hallway and started up the stairs. At the top, she found a bathroom, a small office to the one side and the bedroom on the other. Entering the bedroom first, she looked at the bed the woman had been found in, pushed down on it, and found it moving.

'Water bed,' said Hope, 'well, that's kinky, isn't it?'

'I think that's the best way to describe her, isn't it?' said Dolan. 'I mean, she's not some sort of sex addict or anything; everything is just a little bit kinky. Guess there's people are like that, just like their private life to have a wee bit more fun.'

'What do we know about her private life?' asked Hope.

'Not a lot. We're also not sure what she did for a living.

33

There's been nothing obvious.'

'Have you checked in to any of her bank accounts?'

'Well, no, this has been a health authority investigation; it's not been the police. We've assisted with getting into places, but we haven't had a chance to suspect foul play. It's been just the health officials to prove that.'

'Oh, I understand,' said Hope. 'The boss seems to think it might be different.'

'With all due respect to your boss,' said Sergeant Dolan, 'he's using his intuition going at it with his nose, and he's now got a second death; we didn't. We had somebody that died in her sleep, possibly from food poisoning. We weren't able to find anything she was actually poisoned with.'

'We're not having a go,' said Hope. 'It's just the boss, he has this nose, and when it's on the go, it's on the go. He's rarely wrong.'

'Remember, this is written down into the operations book, DI Macleod's nose says so.'

Hope was ready to fight back and tell the woman to stop being so sharp but Hope probably deserved it. After all, Dolan didn't know Macleod the way Hope did. Hope looked down beside the bed and found a pile of books. She started looking through them, and then pulled her phone out, typing the titles and the authors into an online search. As she got through about the eighth book, she suddenly realised that a lot of the books were erotic thrillers. She opened the pages, looked inside, and held the book open for Dolan.

'It's hardly surprising, is it?' said Dolan. 'It's not like I haven't read the odd book like that myself, back when I was younger. A bit much for a forty-year-old though, isn't it?'

'Not from what I hear,' said Hope. 'I hear a lot of the older women like them.'

Dolan raised her eyebrows, shook her head, and moved out of the room. Hope never stopped, turning round and round, and then she realised why she felt as if the room was bigger than it should have been. She looked up and saw the mirror on the ceiling. *Well, well*, she thought, *I'm no stranger to enjoying my time with men but you really go for it, don't you?*

Next, Hope wemt to the bathroom, where she found a sumptuous bath and a rather bland room otherwise. However, the bath had a Jacuzzi setting. Along the wall, sat bottles that could produce bubbles and scents.

'Certainly liked to pamper herself,' said Hope.

'Maybe,' said Dolan, but this isn't getting us anywhere.'

Hope strode into the small office, looking around and at the computer that sat on the tiny desk. Otherwise, the office had very little in it except more books.

'There's a couple of authors she really likes, isn't there? Look at that shelf at the top,' said Hope, pointing towards the collection of at least sixty books. 'Three names there, only three names. Who are CJ Truss, R Thrust, B Comely?' Hope made her way over to the books, pulling them down, 'These aren't next door,' she said, 'None of these authors were in the bedroom.'

'Maybe there's a special collection, but not B Comely. Look at the covers on it,' said Dolan, pulling out one for herself.

Hope went through all of the books. One of them seemed to be a set of romance books, always a man and woman on the front, albeit the man with a bare chest. The next set of books by Thrust showed bikers, each one with a woman on the bike dressed up in leather and lace. The last series, from B Comely, seemed to show bondage positions on every cover. Dolan had to stop herself from laughing.

'What makes people read this stuff?'

'I don't know,' said Hope. 'Maybe it's a bit of fun, but don't you find this strange? She lives alone. Why are these books in here? Why would you not just have them in the bedroom? If they're going to get you excited in any way, you're not going to have them in an office. Something's not right about this,' said Hope. 'Has anybody looked at that computer?'

'No,' said Dolan.

'In that case, we should take it in,' said Hope. 'Get Ross to have a look at it; somewhere there'll be links into her accounts.'

Hope started to pull open the drawer that sat in a set of cupboards beside the computer. As she pulled open the second drawer, she found two large envelopes. Carefully, she pulled out pictures from within each of them, and started looking at the set of men.

'Do you recognise any of these people?' asked Hope, and she put the photographs down in front of Dolan.

'One or two, I think; possibly from the island, yes.'

The photographs had nothing risqué about them, they were simply head and shoulder shots of men staring, looking glam, some happy, but they were of reasonable quality, like something a photographer would take.

'Maybe we should take those, see if we can identify who they are,' said Hope, 'But we'd better play it carefully. With what's happened, we don't want to charge any of the people. These men could have wives. We don't know what's been going on.'

'Well, it doesn't really fit with her other lifestyle, does it?' said Dolan. 'I'm not sure that these are actually part of her vices.'

'No,' said Hope, pulling open the drawer beneath and finding more envelopes. She pulled out some pictures from there, 'These, however, are,' she said.

'Wow,' said Dolan. 'You won't find me doing that sort of thing.'

Hope looked at the photographs, each one an erotic image of Miranda Folly. As she went through them, she turned them over to the back and found a small sticker on the bottom with three different sets of photographers. Hope began to think that maybe these were just part of her fun.

'Come on,' said Dolan, lifting the computer off the desk.

'Hang on a second,' said Hope, writing down some names of authors, and then she took the photographs of the men and of Miranda Folly under her arm. 'Well,' she said, 'this is certainly going to give Macleod a picture, though I'm not sure he's going to like what I found.'

# Chapter 5

Macleod sat in the canteen area at Stornoway Police Station, polishing off some fish and chips that Clarissa had brought round. Behind him, Ross sat with a sausage supper, and Macleod was beginning to get slightly annoyed at the way he kept smacking his lips.

'It's pretty good here, isn't it, sir?'

'It's not bad, Ross. I'm glad you like your supper. Could be a long one so if I was you, I'd have got a fish supper. Get a bit more into you.'

'I prefer to snack through the night, sir.'

'It wouldn't be as healthy, would it?' With that, the conversation closed until Clarissa, after finishing her fish supper, dipped into her bag, and pulled out a large chocolate bar.

'Anyone for pudding?' Macleod shot a look at her. 'What, Seoras? We're going to be here through the night. I'm going to get some energy into me, aren't I?'

'Never mind that,' said Macleod, 'you and I have got work to do. Ross, we're heading up to the bereaved man's family, to have a word and see what's what. I need to stick my head in and just mention that the circumstances are suspicious. Hopefully, take some heat off the young couple in the coffee house. The last thing we need to do is have anything untoward kicking off.'

'Very good, sir. I've got it covered at this end. Should be expecting McGrath back soon.'

'I'll look forward to the briefing when I get back,' said Macleod. 'Come on, Clarissa,' he said, standing up sharply. Clarissa reached down, picked up her bag, turned around, and noticed that a large chunk of her chocolate bar was missing.

'Eye on the ball,' said Macleod to his sergeant, munching heavily on some chocolate.

Donald 'Tubes' MacDonald lived in Stornoway, up a hill towards the War Memorial in a white house on one side of a long street. From the outside, the house looked like a three-bedroom. As Macleod strode down the driveway, he could see the significant extensions at the rear. As he came to the front door, a police constable gave Macleod a nod and opened it for him. Stepping inside, Macleod looked around and saw the liaison officer given to the family and waved her over quickly while he stood in the hall.

'Constable Diane Macleod.'

'How are we doing?'

'In honesty, I think the wife's holding up pretty well. First name of Donella. She's had a bit of a time of it with seven kids in the family. The younger ones are up in bed. There are three older ones out the back. To be honest, the house is like a rabbit warren, and I can't keep up, but she seems to be running on simply doing things. Some of the family have come over and I'm not sure that's been helpful. There's also been quite a bit of talk about him being food poisoned by the cafe. I've told them inquiries are continuing that we're not saying for definite what's happened. We're still looking into it, but to be

39

honest, I think it's falling on deaf ears.'

'Don't you worry about that,' said Macleod. 'You keep doing your job, keep the family informed, try to smooth the woman's passage through these next couple of days. It won't be easy, but thank you, Constable.'

Macleod entered the living room and saw a tall, thin woman with blonde hair sitting on a sofa. Beside her was a face that looked like a carbon copy, but it was on a woman who was much larger, with dark brown hair. Macleod recognised her sister.

'Donnella MacDonald, my name is Detective Inspector Macleod. This is Detective Sergeant Urquhart. We've come over from the mainland to investigate the death of your husband.'

'Don't you mean murder?' said the sister.

'No, I don't,' said Macleod. 'I am very sorry for your loss, but at this time I am classifying it as simply a suspicious death until I have more detail and I'm able to advise what has actually happened. That's what I'll call it, and that's what I'd like you to think of it as.'

'But it's just the same as Miranda Folly, isn't it? She was poisoned by that place. Now he's been poisoned as well. Sat in the place as well. What more evidence do you need?'

'Excuse me, can I ask your name, ma'am,' said Macleod.

'Murdina,' said the woman. 'I'm Donnella's older sister.'

'Right, Murdina,' said Macleod. 'The fact of it is, it's not open and shut. Simply because Mr MacDonald died in the Cortado Club does not mean they had actually anything to do with it. Until I can find out what killed him, I'll keep a very open mind. It does, however, appear that he probably was poisoned, and my officers are working on that at the moment, trying to determine exactly what it was that unfortunately killed Mr MacDonald.' Macleod turned back to Mrs MacDonald. 'How are you coping at the moment?'

Donella MacDonald looked up. 'I'm just managing, Inspector. It's just the children . . .'

'How do you think she's coping? She's a mess,' said Murdina out loud. 'It's all right; she's allowed to fall apart. It's a terrible thing. But we could do with less questions and you getting on and sorting out these people.'

'I hope you don't mind my asking,' said Macleod, 'but I feel that you could be quite helpful here. Would you step outside, Murdina, and answer a few questions from my Detective Sergeant?'

'What sort of questions do you want to ask me?'

'Just about how you knew your brother-in-law, things like that. Most helpful. I'll just have a little word here with your sister.'

'Well, if you think it's important.'

'I think it could be very instrumental in helping us deal with this issue.'

Macleod watched Murdina stand up and she marched past with an air of self-importance out to the hallway. He felt the tap on his shoulder and Clarissa whispered in his ear.

'What questions are you thinking I should be asking her?'

'You can ask her about the state of the economy. You can ask her about whether she thought *Mister Ed* was a rather good TV program or indeed what her favourite muppet is. Just keep that woman out of this room while I'm asking the questions.'

'Okay, Seoras,' whispered Clarissa, 'but you're going to owe me a bar of chocolate for this.'

'You keep that woman out of my hair and you can have one

41

of those Christmas packs.'

Macleod turned back to Donella MacDonald, his face taking on a serious look. 'I wonder if you could tell me how often your husband frequented the Cortado club?'

'Well, it was his favourite. He liked his coffee, a big lover of coffee. If you go out into our kitchen, Inspector, you'll see it. He has packets of it all up in the cupboard. Even when he wasn't down there, he would come back here, grind up his coffee. He loved it.'

'Was he a connoisseur then?' asked Macleod.

'Well, he liked it. I wouldn't say he was a connoisseur; it wasn't like you could put a cup of coffee in front of him and he could tell you where it came from. He just liked the different tastes, but he was no expert. But he spent a lot of time there. Every day, he'd pop in. He said it was where he liked to do his thinking.'

'What is it that he did for work?'

'He advised people on where to put their money, Inspector, and he was good at it. He took people's cash, put into investments, take a bit back off the top, and he gave them their profit. People seem to think he was good at it, and it all paid for the extensions.'

'And the two of you got on well?'

'We have seven kids, Inspector. You don't have seven kids if you don't get on well; you cut and run after two.'

'I've never had kids,' said Macleod, 'but I'll keep that under advisement. Back to his coffee, when he went down to the Cortado Club, you said he was down for a while. How often and for how long?'

'Like I said, every day, at least two hours. Sometimes it would be longer. He'd maybe make a call to me and he'd say that things had extended. He was on a call when he was having his coffee, and then he had more work to do. Either that or somebody called him, and he had to think through exactly how we make the investments.'

'It didn't bother you, him being down there.'

'Oh, he had an office here, but people need to get out, don't they? Besides, I have my children running around. He was a good father. The best, in fact. He'd come back every evening when they came back from school and spend time with them. That was what he did, you see. He went out, got his work done, came back, spent the time with us.'

'This might seem a strange question, but do you know if he had any enemies?'

'What do you mean?'

'When he did these investments, did any ever go wrong? Did he ever say to you that people were upset with him?'

'No. He didn't talk much about the work to me.'

'What did he do outside of work?' asked Macleod. 'Was he part of the Rotary Club? Did he go bowling? Things like that.'

'He didn't. It was all the family, ours and his extended family. Murdina, my sister, her kids, he was into them all. He wasn't just a great father; he was a great uncle. On Sunday, we'd all go down to the church together, we'd sit together, we'd take up two rows. He had three brothers, a sister. I have two sisters, two brothers. It's an extensive family we have.

'So I hear,' said Macleod. 'Have they all been through here tonight?'

'A lot of them have called. They haven't all been here.'

'Does your family believe that he was food poisoned?'

'Well, what else is there? I don't understand why you're asking me that. Surely, you'll confirm that.'

'I'll confirm if that's the case. If it's not, then I'll tell you something else. That's why I'm asking. At the moment I'm treating the death of your husband as suspicious, not as an open and shut case. Did he ever have any money worries?' asked Macleod. The woman shook her head. 'Any illnesses? Did he have any health issues that would cause him to believe he wouldn't live long?'

'No, Inspector. He was in good health. I mean, he had a little bit of a belly on him, but that's just fatherhood isn't it?'

Macleod looked down and realised that fatherhood was yet to come upon him, although Jane was doing her best with what she fed him.

'So, you cannot think of any reason why anyone would want to harm him?'

'No. You can call the family, ask them. Everyone loved him. He was great; he didn't hurt anyone. I mean, we're at the church every Sunday. We have a good church life, and we basically get involved with our kids and their clubs. With their lives, we're everywhere. If he was doing anything, he was working for them or he was raising money. That's the sort of person my husband was.'

Macleod looked around the living room and saw plenty of photographs. They were faces he recognised. The deceased man, Donella, her sister. On display were a lot of family portraits.

'Well, I'm going to think further at the moment,' said Macleod. 'But let me extend my condolences to you. I'll try and disturb you as little as possible because I know this is a rough time for you. However, I may need to come back and ask more questions. One thing I would say is, do not go near the Cortado Club. There's been a little bit of trouble down there tonight already. Somebody put a rock through the window calling the owners murderers. Nothing is proven, and until it is, I'd rather not find my case being skewed. If it does turn out that for some reason, they managed to poison your husband, let the law do its work. Again, my condolences for your loss.'

Macleod took his leave of the room, walked out into the hall, and shouted down it, 'Time to go, DS Urquhart.'

'Yes, sir,' came the reply. Macleod was stunned to hear the footsteps of Clarissa as soon as he stepped out of the door, following him.

'You owe me big for that one, Seoras. Man, that woman can talk.'

'What did you ask her about?'

'Family,' said Clarissa. 'Just family. And she went on and on. Do you know how many are in their family? I'm not being funny; there must be over fifty names there.'

'Did you write them down?'

'Every one of them. Well, you did say to keep her occupied.'

'That I did, but there's something bothering me. Just a second.' Macleod picked up his mobile and rang Stornoway police station. After the call was answered, he was put through to Ross, in the operations room.

'Ross, have you gone through the statements made by the owners?'

'I was looking over them again, sir. Why? What do you need?'

'Our deceased man, Mr MacDonald. What do they have to say about him?'

'In what way?'

'Well, how long was he there?'

'You mean when he visits?'

45

'Yes, and how often does he visit?'

'Hang on, sir.' Macleod waited in silence, turned about, and looked at the white house, admiring the extensions that had been put onto the rear. You would hardly know from the front, so clearly, Mr MacDonald was not ostentatious.

'Sir, it seems from their statements, he's there roughly about forty minutes, but just about every day.'

'Just check what they said. Forty minutes?'

'Yes, sir. I'm reading it here. At the most, he would be in for forty minutes.'

'Where does that statement come from?' asked Macleod.

'Well, Boris says it, and yes, Alison says it as well, but separately. We took statements from them, and they were completed by two separate police constables who interviewed them. He's there for forty minutes a day.'

'That's interesting,' said Macleod, 'because I just spoke to his wife, and he's usually there for at least two hours. She agrees he visits every day, but for at least two hours and sometimes for longer.'

'That's not tallying up, sir,' said Ross. 'I guess it's going to be quite important to find out where he is the rest of the time.'

'Do you think, Ross?' said Macleod. 'How about looking up how long Miranda Folly was there for?'

'It's not here but hang on, just let me bring something up.' Macleod could hear Ross typing away in the background. 'I'm just bringing up from the other investigation; some of the constables interviewed owners at the potential sites for food poisoning, and I think they interviewed Boris. Just a second. Yes, here it is. Oh,' he said, 'Miranda. She only stays about forty minutes.'

'Now, that is interesting,' said Macleod. 'We have two dead

people, both of whom frequent the same coffee house, both of whom go most days, and both of whom seem to stay for roughly the same amount of time.'

'Sounds a bit more than a coincidence, sir,' said Ross.

'Yes,' said Macleod. It really does.'

# Chapter 6

Hope McGrath looked over at her boss. His feet were up on the table as he lay back in a chair, his head tipped to one side. The eyes were closed, and she could hear him snoring lightly. He'd dropped off only ten minutes ago. Clarissa went to speak to him but when she got close, Hope put a hand up and indicated that his other sergeant leave him alone.

'Give him an hour,' she'd said to Clarissa. The trouble with arriving in a crime scene such as this was that Macleod always wanted to get on the go. Just like every other time, he would usually work through the night until he came up with a line of inquiry. He was also waiting on Jona Nakamura who was working through the night up at the hospital to see if she could produce some results about how the deceased were killed.

Earlier on in the evening, Hope advised Macleod what she had found at Miranda Folly's house. The inspector agreed that it was a good course of inquiry to check into the woman's bank records, especially now that Macleod had put a connection, at least coincidentally, between Miranda and Donald MacDonald.

Ross was looking into the account in the way only Ross

could and Hope felt she was kicking about. She would read through, time and again, the statements made to the police constables. She wasn't really in a position at this time to go off hurtling into the night, pulling people away from their beds, as somebody had already interviewed them about when they went to a cafe. She tried to help Ross with coordinating who was in the cafe at the time. She debriefed Clarissa at one point, extracting her view of what had happened. Hope knew this was just killing time until Ross had come up with information about Miranda Folly.

Hope was getting fed up with waiting. She walked behind Ross's back, going backwards and forwards, looking at his screen from time to time as the man punched in more digits and pulled up record after record.

'You could walk around the back of me all night but until I'm ready, I'm not going to speak about it.'

'Hey, I'm your boss,' said Hope. 'If I want you to speak about it, I'll tell you to speak about it.'

'Well, you can but I don't have anything to speak about until I finish. But…' Ross tapped an empty cup.

'Only because it's you,' said Hope, laughing. She picked up his cup and made her way over to a filter coffee machine that had been placed there just that night. Sergeant Dolan made sure Macleod had the one thing that kept him going and Hope had thanked her for it. Dolan had gone home, and the night watch had come in. Macleod seconded a few people to him. More would be seconded in the morning as he had asked Dolan to try to contact those who were either on holiday or those who were just simply off, to see if they wanted the overtime.

Hope set the coffee down beside Ross and as she went to walk away, he looked up at his redheaded boss. 'Stay,' he said, 'please. I need to take you through a little journey here. You can stay and enjoy the last bit with me.'

'What do you mean?' asked Hope

'Well, look,' said Ross. 'I've gone into her bank accounts. If you look at the screen, here,' and he pointed to a number of digits on the screen, 'trace them across and you'll see that she gets payment from Amazon, Kobo, and a lot of other big distributers. They are for self-publishers. People who are not traditionally published.'

'Okay. So what?'

'Well, if you look at it, look at the money coming in.'

'That's bigger than my salary,' said Hope.

'Yep,' said Ross. 'That's one of them. Look at the others. They're there too. I think Miranda's got a business account somewhere. Yep, here it is. There'll be serious money in that as well. That's a business account,' said Ross. 'Serious money in it.'

'But she doesn't look like a woman with money.'

'No, she doesn't, or she didn't. I'm going to contact these distributers because I want to find out what she publishes. Trouble is I can't do it from the screen. Just give me a moment.'

Hope sat down in a chair opposite Ross as he picked up the phone. She watched him dial a number. He got through, waited for twenty minutes, and was told somebody else needed to help him. He was put through to someone else. He was then given a number to call, which Ross duly did. At this point, Hope stood up, went outside, and walked around the block before coming back in. She felt herself growing tired. The eyes had been closing and she felt that the cold air would pick her up. When she came back, Ross was still on the phone.

'You're not done yet?' asked Hope, but all she got was a finger up in her face indicating she should stay quiet.

'Hello, this is Detective Constable Ross from Inverness Police Station. I've been looking into the records of one Miranda Folly, and they indicate that she has an account with you for which you pay a significant amount of money each year. Perhaps this month. What I'd like to know is her pen names. I was told by various people in your company that you could do this.'

'Do you know what time of hour it is?' said a voice on the other end of the phone.

'Yes, I do,' said Ross. 'I apologise for it. To be quite frank, I haven't stopped today. And I'm not going to stop until the sun comes up because I'm involved in a murder investigation. Would you kindly advise me of the information that I've asked?'

'Murder investigation?' said the voice on the other end. 'Ooh, and you're the police?'

'Detective Constable Ross. I don't think I'm asking you for anything ridiculous. I just want to know Miranda Folly's pen names because she's obviously selling books. If you could advise me the genre, even better.'

'Stand by,' said the voice. Ross looked across at Hope, shaking his shoulders. Hope yawned and got something thrown out at her from across the room.

'Don't start the yawning stuff,' said Clarissa. 'I didn't get this when I worked on the art side. Middle of the night stuff and he's still asleep,' said Clarissa pointing at Macleod.

Hope laughed but then she saw Ross motioning for everyone to be quiet again. 'Okay, the names then: CJ Truss, R Thrust, B Comely. Is that it? Lovely. Well, thank you for your help. Yes, it is ridiculous hour of the night. Many thanks.'

Hope stood up and walked over to Ross. 'Did you just say—?'

'Yes, I did,' said Ross. 'Truss, Thrust, and Comely. I believe you wrote those names down, didn't you?'

'Yes. But they're all—'

'They're all Miranda Folly.'

'So, you're telling me that Miranda Folly was an author, but not only that, but she was writing erotica.'

'Well, let's have a look,' said Ross typing names into the Amazon website. 'Yes, you see there.'

'That's all erotic, isn't it? She was earning money from this,' said Hope.

'She was earning good money from it. I don't know why you're surprised about that. Many people earn money this way, a lot of them making very good money.'

'But why wasn't she well known?'

'Let me find out,' said Ross. He come back to his phone, dialling a number.

'Hi, there. Yes, it's Alan. Sorry to bother you.'

Hope realised that Ross was onto one of his friends. It was a bit crazy phoning them at this hour, but she wasn't going to interrupt Ross when he'd gone to do it directly.

'Really?' said Ross. Hope tried to listen in. 'That's remarkable. When was that?' Hope watch Ross making some notes. It was ten minutes before the conversation was finished. Ross turned and smiled at his boss.

'You're not going to believe this. She's not just somebody who earns money from writing erotic and novels. She is one of the top erotic novel writers.'

'No way. She's here on the Isle of Lewis.'

'Yes,' said Ross. 'You want to know why she keeps stuff quiet?'

'I can't see it going down well here. Do we know how long she's been writing that sort of stuff?'

52

'You said her house contained quite a few items?'

'Yes, nothing ridiculous. Wasn't like she had a whole dungeon set up in the basement or anything,' said Hope. 'But she definitely liked the erotic side.'

'Well,' said, Ross. 'There's a reason for that, she makes good money out of it. I was just talking to my friend, Francesco; he's into these things as well. He says that she's been big now for about five or six years and she's actually appeared at conventions in America. Now, the thing is that they don't generally tend to put their picture on the back of anything, but she's gone over to America where clearly, people want to know her, but people from here are not going to.'

'That gives another angle to this, doesn't it?'

'In what way?'

'Well, an erotica queen on the Isle of Lewis.'

Hope heard the thud and saw Macleod's feet had fallen off the desk. He was sat up in the chair, his eyes wide open.

'There's a what in Stornoway?'

'Nobody said Stornoway,' said Hope. 'Just the Isle of Lewis.'

'There's a what?' asked Macleod again.

'It turns out, sir,' said Ross, 'that Miranda Folly was an erotic writer. She's very big as well, earning money that is apparently far greater than Sergeant McGrath's salary. She's been doing it for five or six years. She goes over to America, where she's very well known, but it seems that nobody knows her here.'

'When you say erotica, what do you mean?'

'Well, you know, sexual content,' said Ross.

'No,' said Macleod. 'Of course, I know it means that. What sort of level?

'Well, Sergeant McGrath is the one for that. She's had a look at a few of her books.'

Hope saw Macleod's stare. 'They were in the house,' said Hope quickly. 'I don't read them normally.'

'I believe you, thousands wouldn't. What were they like?' asked Macleod.

Hope felt herself beginning to flush, going slightly red. She had no idea why. Why should she be embarrassed to talk about this? When she'd first met Macleod, he was the one who would've been embarrassed.

'Well, some of them were more on the romantic side, some heading towards the bondage side of things.'

'Things you would say that the island would struggle with?' asked Macleod.

'Well, I'm sure it's here if you remember our first case.'

'I know it's here,' said Macleod. 'I have no dreamy thoughts about my home. Of course, it's here, but there's a difference between things being here and being tolerated or frowned upon. There are things here in the shadows that in other places like the cities, would be out in the open.'

'You think it might give somebody a motive to kill her?'

'I don't think anything,' Macleod said to Ross. 'What I do think is it makes her a very interesting woman. I have a very interesting woman who spends the same time at a certain coffee house as a man who's deceased as well. Now, this man tells his wife he's only going there for a certain period of time. However, that period of time is far longer than he actually spends in the coffee shop. He actually spends the same amount of time as a woman who is into things that might not be seen in a good light on this island.'

'You think they're an item?' asked Ross.

'Let's not jump forward, Ross. All I'm saying is there's a lot of coincidences here that we need to look at. Any word from

54

Jona yet?'

'No,' said Hope. 'She said she'd call as soon as she had something.'

'It's quite key because, at the moment, we've got a suspicious death. We don't know if it's a murder or not, both of them. If it was a murder, the things we've just talked about, they become very important. If it's just a suspicious death where somebody's been poisoned by food, it becomes some bizarre facts for journalists to play with.'

'The wife didn't say anything about her husband enjoying that side of things.'

'No, Ross. She didn't. I wasn't exactly about to barge in and ask, even if I had known the detail from Hope. She portrayed him as a family man, wholesome, terrific image. It's an image I recognise very well on this island, one a lot of people put up. But most probably don't turn out to be people who like sex and activity with other people. Most merely like a drink or are just not that nice with other people. But this one, this intrigues me. By the way, is there any coffee there?'

'Yes,' said Clarissa. 'I filled it up while you were asleep.'

'Asleep?' queried Macleod. 'Oh, I wasn't asleep. I heard every word.' He stood up and made his way over to the filter coffee machine.

Hope bent down and whispered in Ross's ear. 'He was never awake. That coffee machine's been on for an hour. He would have leapt at it.'

# Chapter 7

Macleod received word from Jona Nakamura, the forensic lead of the team, that she'd be down at the station at approximately six o'clock. Hearing the information, Macleod made a direct line for the canteen to make sure he had breakfast before she arrived. The rest of the team took the hint as well. By the time Jona came through the door, the morning shift of constables and sergeants were making their way in. When Jona had set up in the investigation room to give her briefing, it had become a flurry of activity with some of the night shifts staying on to hear her before they went home.

Macleod sat across from her at the side of the room, Hope beside him, while the rest remained behind tables and chairs, waiting for the diminutive Asian woman to start.

'I'm sorry, it's taken me a while, but I wanted to be absolutely sure,' said Jona. 'I have conducted an autopsy on both victims to see why they died. The second victim, Donald MacDonald, has clearly been poisoned with thallium.'

'Thallium?' queried Macleod.

'Yes, thallium. Quite straightforward in some ways, administered in a large dose, it was ingested, and it took the man a couple of hours to die. I found residue of it still in his stomach. The other victim, Miranda Folly, was harder to deduce, although it was thallium as well. Once I understood that was how Mr MacDonald had died and went looking for it in Miranda Folly, there were very small traces within her stomach. I can't say what the quantity was to begin with, but I would suspect that that is what killed her. I cannot find any other reason.

'Thallium—you wouldn't taste it, would you?' asked Macleod.

'Taste it, no. It's liquid, it's colourless. In some ways, it's the poisoners' poison,' said Jona. 'On the other hand, it's also quite well known. You don't have to do much research to find it as an ideal substance with which to murder someone. The quantity you'd have to put in would be reasonable enough; otherwise, the subject would recover albeit having gone through quite a rough time. Both our subjects died; therefore, I'm suspecting a reasonable quantity was added.'

'If it was put into coffee,' asked Macleod, 'would that mean it was covered over? Would you even begin to taste it when you drank it?'

'I would suspect not. You wouldn't see it in the coffee either,' said Jona.

'Would the liquid spill out of the top, though,' asked Hope, 'out of a cup?'

'That's a good point,' said Macleod.

'Also,' said Ross 'if you administered it into the coffee, wouldn't you see where it went then?'

'Like a hole or something you mean.'

'There's nothing to say that it had to be administered before somebody started to drink it,' said Jona. 'You can add it halfway through somebody having a cup, that wouldn't be a problem.'

'The suspects, perhaps, and the deceased were there for quite a while in the coffee shop,' said Dolan, 'if that's the line we're going down.'

'It's not the line we're specifically going,' said Macleod; 'it's just a line of inquiry.'

'You think the owners added it?'

'I don't think anybody added it. I don't know at the moment. I'm still struggling to work out why people would want to kill what seemed to be a perfect family man and a woman who lived on her own. She didn't seem to have any enemies, neither did he. However, we have some circumstantial evidence that's tying them together when they go for these coffees, and that stays in this room.'

Macleod looked across the room in front of him and saw some hurt faces. 'There's no need for that,' said Macleod. 'I know this island. I'm from here. I'm just like the rest of you, but I also know the rumour mill that it is. The last thing we need is any lines of inquiry becoming rumour, especially as we could get them wrong. It's unhelpful so make sure we keep this tight.' Macleod's glare went across the room, and Clarissa felt she had to say something.

'We get it, boss, don't worry. I'm sure we all get it.'

Macleod looked back at Jona, indicating that she should continue.

'There's not really much more to say,' said Jona. 'As I said, I looked through on my autopsy, I can't find anything else, I can't find any indications of violence towards them. Both seemed to be in reasonable health outside of being poisoned. I can't find any other reason why they would be dead. If the poison was added, it wasn't in a forceful manner. In other words, there's no indications that their mouth was held open, that it was put into them with their knowledge.'

'The time delays are okay. You could effectively have put this poison in, what, twelve hours before they were found?'

'Twelve hours before they died, Inspector,' said Jona. 'That would certainly be reasonable in the first case. The difficulty with Miranda Folly is I don't know in what quantity it was added. Obviously, it was enough to kill her, but depending on the quantity you added, you can speed up the time of death. It's not an exact science. There are several factors.'

'It would have been that day,' said Macleod.

'Oh, yes. It certainly would have been that day.'

'If Donald MacDonald was poisoned in the cafe, it would have had to be a hefty dose.'

'Yes. When I say a hefty dose, I'm not saying you have to pour it in by the bucket load, but it's more than a drop.'

'To sum up,' said Macleod, 'we believe they were both killed by thallium poisoning, and we believe it happened on the day. With Donald MacDonald, it quite possibly happened while he was at the cafe alone. It would have to have been enough of a dose, but you're saying from what you found, the residue was enough, but that's a possibility.'

'Yes,' said Jona, 'very much a possibility. I can't say so much about Miranda Folly. It's been quite a while. Obviously, the longer before I get to the body, the more it can change, and things become harder to ascertain.'

'Thank you,' said Macleod, and turned to his team, dismissing the rest of the room. Clarissa and Ross came over, huddling around the desk Macleod sat on, while Hope perched on the edge of it.

'What are we thinking?' asked Macleod.

59

'Well, I know what you're thinking,' said Clarissa. 'You're thinking they're dumping it in the coffee. You can't say that for sure.'

'No, I can't,' said Macleod. 'That's why I told everyone we are running our line of inquiry, but what we can say is, we've got a close connection between the two victims, and one of those connections is that coffee house.'

'We need to get into the owners,' said Hope, 'see if they had a reason to despise these people.'

'Indeed,' said Macleod. 'Ross, you need to check their backgrounds, but we also need something else.'

'What do you mean?' asked Hope.

'I think we're going to need to work out who had the opportunity of being in that shop. They would be there, having coffee, and could move about, and calmly drop thallium into the coffee. The owners, obviously, have ample opportunity, so do the staff, but there are other people there. Do people go over and chat? How do they do it? If you added a significant quantity, would the liquid pool at the top of the cup? What do these people drink? How do they drink it? Did they drink it fast? Slow? Where did they sit with their coffee in front of them? Who moved about? These are all things you need to get into.'

'Do they have CCTV there?' asked Ross.

'No,' said Clarissa. 'There wasn't any of that. They had a camera up in the corner, but it's a dummy pointed at the till anyway. It wasn't pointed out at the shop.'

'Blast,' said Macleod. 'I could have wrapped this up quite quickly.'

'What do we make of our victims though?' asked Hope. 'It all seems a bit strange. Are we sure we're connecting them together correctly?'

'Oh, a family man. Model churchman as well,' said Clarissa, 'What do you think, Seoras? You're from here.'

'Well, there's plenty of men here like that. Good men,' said Seoras. 'There's also a lot of covering up going on. People who want to portray an image.'

'Oh, he is certainly a randy one,' said Clarissa; 'seven kids.'

'He's a what?' blurted Macleod.

'Randy, sir. Likes it a lot. You know what I mean, Seoras.'

'He and his wife wanted to start a large family. That's a bit of a jump.'

'It's not really,' said Hope. 'Maybe that home wasn't enough. Maybe he's an addict of some sort.'

'Out of due diligence to keep an open mind,' began Macleod, 'I'll say that's a possibility, but we haven't got anything on the man. The hard thing is going to be getting a true picture. They're a large family, and they're going to back him to the hilt. We've already seen someone come down to the corner of the shop window and smash it in. I'm reckoning that's friends and family.'

'Spoke to the constables on last night, sir. No more activity on that front,' advised Clarissa.

The phone rang in the office and one of the constables picked it up, looked across and he waved towards Macleod who pointed at Clarissa, asking her to take it.

'It was not the owner,' said Macleod. 'We need to find the other punters and then we need to get background on them. This is going to be a case of digging in, talking to everyone. It's going to be a lot of groundwork on this one.'

'Well, we can go out and interview them once we know who is who,' said Hope.

'Dolan's in again today, isn't she?' asked Macleod.

'I think so.'

'Good. You need to bring her in then. Let me go down and talk to the shop staff, whoever's down at the shop if they come in today, otherwise out to their house, find out who frequents the shop, how and when they frequent it. That's the next line of attack.'

'Detective Inspector,' shouted Clarissa across the room.

*Detective Inspector* thought Macleod. *Not Seoras. Must be important.* He stood up and made his way across to the phone.

'It's the shop owners,' said Clarissa. 'They're wanting to know if they can open up today.'

Macleod took the phone from her, giving her a grim stare. 'Hello. This is D I Macleod.'

'Inspector, this is Boris. Can we open the shop today? You said yesterday, we should close, but I don't see why not.'

'I can't stop you from opening it,' said Macleod, 'but I think given the heated tensions, that you would be unwise to. Somebody put a rock through your window last night.'

'Yes, but I need to work. I need to bring money in.'

'You're not worried that people are going to stay away from your coffee house, associating it with poisonings?'

'Poisonings? We did not food poison anyone. Most people will know that. Have you ever heard of food poisoning from coffee?' asked Boris.

'Indeed, sir. Well, I can't stop you and it's up to you, but my advice is not to. However, I will advise the constables at your shop that they're more than welcome to let you in, but I would say one thing: be careful. If you do get any more instances like last night, I would stop.'

'Thank you, Inspector. I'll think about that if it happens.'

'I'll also be dropping in,' said Macleod. 'I need to speak to you and your staff.'

'About what?' asked Boris. 'I thought you did all the interviews.'

'We did, but I need to speak to you. It's one thing to go off what you've said to other people, but I need to understand that coffee shop and how things happened.'

'Why?' asked Boris.

'There's a possibility that both of the deceased were poisoned in your cafe.'

'I told you my food, it is fine. The coffee, it is fine. You don't get poisoned in a coffee house.'

'Not by the food, not by the coffee,' said Macleod. 'We know now that both victims were poisoned, sir, in which case I am looking at murder. With that in mind, be very careful.' The phone went quiet on the other end until the man spoke up.

'I understand, Inspector, but I need to open. I need the money. Do you understand?'

'Yes,' said Macleod, 'but you have my advice. It is up to you.' Macleod put the phone down and stared off at the far wall. He tried to work out Boris's reaction. When he said that they'd been murdered, he didn't seem to bat much of an eyelid. He simply went quiet before saying he had to work. Is the man just preoccupied with his own troubles or had he known about it all along?

Hope appeared on his shoulder. 'What's the matter, boss?'

'They want to open up the coffee house again. I've just told them we think that our two victims may have been murdered there and he wants to open. He's had a stone put through the window and he wants to open. He's either desperately short of cash or—'

63

'Or he's in on it,' said Hope, 'in some shape or fashion. Does this change your plans?'

'No,' said Macleod. 'No. I still think this is going to be something where we're going to have to go on the ground and talk. Let's look at the time,' said Macleod. 'Nearly eight o'clock. I think they open at nine. I think it'll be time to go for a coffee then. What do you think, Hope?'

'I've never had a cortado,' said Hope. 'What is it?'

'Double ristretto,' said Macleod. 'Silky milk, a little bit of fluff, and by the looks of it, a touch of thallium as well.'

# Chapter 8

'Ross is not going to be happy with you,' said Hope. 'He's doing what he's good at. Ross is better with the numbers on the computer screens.'

'Yes, but he's missing out on the coffee,' said Hope as they walked down to the coffee shop, Clarissa in tow.

'It's not like I'm popping out for a quick drink,' said Macleod. 'This is work. We're investigating.'

'And you're not going to try the coffee? That'll be a first for you,' said Hope.

'I can get one, though, can't I?' said Clarissa.

Macleod flung her a look. 'I suppose you'll be wanting one as well, Sergeant Dolan.'

'On duty, sir? Of course not.'

Macleod gave the woman a smile and continued to walk the short distance from the police station down to the coffee shop. He stopped outside and looked up, seeing the Cortado Club sign emblazoned across the top of the shop, the windows underneath, and a man standing there taking the window out and putting a new pane in.

'That's fast work,' said Macleod.

'I didn't think you had that sort of thing here on the island,' said Clarissa.

'We're not barbarians,' said Macleod, 'but that is fast work. I might ask him about that one.'

Macleod strode inside checking his watch and realising the time was now half past nine. He had intended to come half an hour earlier, but he thought it best to let the shop get into its own routine, so you could start to see it as it really was. He approached the front counter where Boris attended him.

'Inspector, can I get you anything?'

'I'll have a cortado,' said Macleod. 'Detective Sergeant Urquhart will have one as well. However, I'm not sure my other two colleagues think it's appropriate that we should drink coffee on the job.'

'Enough of that,' said Hope.

'Four cortados,' said Macleod. 'We'll just sit over there. When you've got a moment, I'd like to have a word with you.'

'Of course, Inspector.' Macleod sat down on a comfy sofa. Clarissa took a position beside him on the opposite side of the table beside Hope and Sergeant Dolan.

'What are you doing, Seoras?' asked Hope.

'I'm watching how they make this. I'm watching what they do behind the counter because looking at what they're doing at the moment, you'd have to be pretty nifty to drop something in. Real sleight-of-hand job.'

'You'd also have people standing at the counter waiting to order,' said Clarissa. 'There's no guarantee you're going to get any sort of privacy and if you're operating with the staff not knowing, well, look at them. There's three people behind there in that area. It's crowded. You're not going to have a hope, are you?'

'I wouldn't go that far,' said Macleod. 'But it would be tough,

66

difficult. Probably done at a time when it was quieter if you were going to do it.'

A few minutes later, one of the serving staff arrived. He placed a tray down on the table then lifted off four saucers with cortados and placed one in front of each of them.

'Well, cheers to you all,' said Macleod. 'Let's get to the bottom of this,' and he took a sip of his coffee.

A few moments later Boris came over, standing beside him. 'How busy are you at the moment?' asked Macleod.

'There's an initial rush and then there's a lull for a bit before the mid-morning coffee drinkers come in,' said Boris. 'If you want to talk, now is good.'

'My sergeant's going to go and talk to some of your staff as well. We're looking to get a picture of the place but please sit down so I can talk to you.'

Hope and Dolan stood up and along with Clarissa began talking to the staff while Boris sat opposite Macleod. Macleod could see his hands, nervy and twitching.

'How are you feeling about things?' asked Macleod.

'It's bad,' said Boris. 'It's bad. We have two people dead. My coffee house is named amongst it. It's bad. We need to make money. We need to get on and do better.'

'How well did you know your customers?'

'I know them from coming in. I mean, I don't know their private life. I know what cup of coffee they like. I can tell you who takes sweetener, who takes sugar. I can tell you who buys coffee for who. We even know what cake they like, but I'm a coffee house. I serve coffee. We have the odd chat. I can tell you what most of them do for a living.'

'Did you know what Miranda Folly did for a living?'

'She never said,' said Boris, 'but she had one of those book things. The electronic ones, Kindle,' he said, 'and she'd bring it out all the time. She liked to read that, but I always thought she read it too much, too closely, too detailed.'

'What do you mean?' asked Macleod.

'Like she was studying it.'

Macleod simply nodded. 'What about the others?'

'Donald MacDonald, he's well known in the island, but I didn't know much about him or what he did. Which of the rest of my customers would you like to know about?'

'Donald's wife said that he came down here most days. Is that correct?'

'Nearly every day. We don't open Sunday.'

*Of course, you don't*, thought Macleod. *Even these days, of course, you didn't.* 'When he came down, did he sit alone?'

'No. Quite often people would be with him.'

'People like who?'

'He had a friend who liked to come and sit. Counsellor Morgan, I think he is. He's quite old, but they were buddies. That's how you say it over here, isn't it? Buddies.'

'So, they would chat for long?'

'He was pretty quick. Most people you expect to stop by for half an hour. Maybe some take an hour if they're talking. Most people if they go beyond an hour will buy a second coffee. Some buy it before then, but he was in forty minutes and gone every time.'

'Who was in when he was in?'

'Say that again.'

'Sorry,' said Macleod. 'Who was in the shop whenever Donald was in the shop?'

'It could be any one of the staff.'

'No, not the staff. The people, customers; what other

customers were in with him?'

'Well, like I say, his friend, counsellor Morgan. He was always there, but he's very well known. Likes to talk to everybody when he's in as well, so he'd sit down, talk to Donald, then he's up and he's talking to so and so and whatever. Yes, he was in.'

'Anybody else you can think?'

'There's a student that comes in,' he said. 'She's here most mornings. She's got the laptop open working. There's a guy that was in the paper. He's here a lot. I think he was in the Island Games. I don't know his name, but he comes in for coffee and a woman Morgan always talked to. In fact, Donald always said hello. Grundy, she is. Very *velceraporpus*.'

'*Velceraporpus?*' said Macleod.

'You know. Big woman.'

'Very voluptuous,' said Macleod.

'Yes, that's it. Big. Cuddly,' said Boris.

Macleod wasn't sure that voluptuous and cuddly really represented the same thing, but he wasn't going to argue.

'Oh, and of course, Annie Spence. Annie's always here, but she's old, little old lady in the corner, Annie. They may be here today if you wait around,' said Boris. 'I don't know. With all that's happened, maybe some will stay away.'

'You're insistent you need to stay open, but from what I can gather, the coffee shop's done very well, Boris.'

'It's doing well, but we had to take a lot of money out to finance it in the start, so it still needs to do well for another year or two until we get back on our feet.'

'Okay,' said Macleod, 'I'll let you get back to your work.'

Boris returned behind the counter and Hope sat down beside Macleod. 'Interesting?' she asked.

'Number of names. How about you?'

'Well, I spoke to Alison, Boris's wife, and she said there was a Sarah MacIver, a student that came in.'

'Boris mentioned her.'

'It seems that she's here every morning. Certainly would have crossed the times that Donald MacDonald would be here.'

'Did Alison say anything about the business?'

'No, but she looked quite annoyed that she was in today. In some ways, she's quite frightened.'

'I would be as well. If somebody was killing off clients within my coffee shop, I would be.'

'She also seemed quite annoyed at her husband.'

'Are they married?' asked Macleod.

'No. He's her partner, technically,' said Hope, 'but they look like a husband and wife.'

'She was annoyed at him though, you said. Why?'

'She doesn't understand why they had to be in today, why they couldn't shut the shop for three or four days.'

'But Boris said it was quite important. They hadn't made enough money, and they'd spent so much since the start, but he needed another year, or two, to be clear.'

'That's not what Alison said. She said things are going really well. She was over the moon. Delighted with what had happened. Her biggest concern was the fact that this was going to ruin them, the broken window, et cetera.'

'How did they get that put back so quick?'

'I don't know,' said Hope. 'Failed to ask that one.'

Clarissa plunked herself down in the sofa opposite the window. 'The guy out front is Alison's uncle. That's why the window is getting done so quick.'

'Well, that's handy,' said Macleod.

'Yes. Just had a word with him. He's livid. He says it's that

70

MacDonald clan that's done it. He said they're all jumping to conclusions. I'll not tell you exactly what he said because you won't like the language, Seoras, but trust me, the man's up in arms.'

'I hope you calmed him down somewhat, told him not to do anything daft.'

'Of course. Soul of discretion, that's me.'

'Good,' said Macleod, 'so what have we got?'

'Just give us a minute,' said Clarissa, 'Sergeant Dolan's just coming back.'

The four of them then, sitting down at the table, began to band about the results of the interviews they'd just conducted.

'So,' said Macleod, 'basically, it's like this. Any time Donald MacDonald was in, we're reckoning that Miranda Folly would have been here. Other people: Sarah MacIver comes in, a student, Innes Stewart.'

'Now, he's a big name,' said Dolan. 'You see, he won a gold medal at the Island Games not that long back. There was a right load of hoo-ha about it because he retained his title two years later. He's also that sort of person, very outgoing, well-known, well-liked, born and bred on the island.'

'Okay,' said Macleod. 'Then we got an Annie Spence.'

'Ah, she's an old one,' said Dolan. 'You see her down the Sally Ann or sauntering round about the street sometimes, in and out. Harmless little soul.'

'We've got Counsellor Morgan, who's a friend of MacDonald's; be interesting to see how he reacts to it all,' said Macleod.

'Now, that's a man who may have enemies,' said Dolan, 'because he's got detractors on the council. He's very much old-school, keeping things the way they were, and often, that's ticked off a few people. I wouldn't see him and Miranda Folly

71

getting on particularly well.'

'And the last one,' said Macleod, 'seems to be a Joy Grundy.'

'Well, that might be up your street, Seoras,' said Hope. 'I was told that she was a local radio celebrity, but also a big church woman.'

'Well, when you say a church woman,' said Dolan, 'she is certainly from the church, but probably the more modern church, very outgoing.'

'Boris said she was *velceraporpus*.'

'What?' said Clarissa.

'Well, I managed to hone him down. It either meant voluptuous, or cuddly.'

'Oh, I get that,' said Dolan, 'I get what he means.'

'In what way?' asked Hope.

'She's a big girl and she's full of life. I say girl—she must be approaching her forties—but she's a force of nature. She does a radio show as well on the Sunday evenings, where people come on and talk about their faith and stuff. She's well-liked. Actually, by both sides. She's not just a religious zealot and seems to cut across, but I do think sometimes she likes being popular.'

'In what way?' asked Macleod.

'Everything she's doing seems to be with her in the limelight. Never heard anybody talk about what she does on the quiet.'

'Well,' said Macleod, 'this is where this line of inquiry is going, so let's see if we can find these people. Hope, I want you to take Annie and Sarah, go see them, find out what connections they've got to our deceased pair. Clarissa, Innes Stuart.'

'Oh, the athlete.'

'No,' says Dolan, 'he's not an athlete. He won his medal for shooting. He's in the gun club.'

Clarissa looked somewhat disappointed. 'And where would I get him?' she asked.

'You might try down Harris. That's where he's from, but he comes up here most days, apparently, and I'll take Joy and Morgan.'

'Picking the extremes then, sir?' said Dolan.

'How do you mean?'

'I'll tell you now, Morgan will be a dry soul and Joy will be all over you.'

'You'll enjoy that, Seoras,' said Clarissa. 'You like a *velcera-porpus* woman.'

'Clarissa, before you go,' said Macleod, his face incredibly serious, 'Cortado for Ross, hand-delivered.'

# Chapter 9

Hope McGrath walked along the streets of Stornoway, looking for the number quoted to her by Ross. Annie Spence was on the electoral register, a widow who lived in a small abode in the centre of Stornoway. The houses were quite small, consisting of maybe three rooms downstairs and two or three upstairs, and Hope realised that the woman certainly wasn't coming from money.

As she reached the correct door, she tried to look in through the window, but there were net curtains and Hope couldn't see through them. She made for the front door, which again was glass but with a curtain hanging down behind it. Hope looked around and saw the cars on the street and doubted that Annie belonged to any of them. She was eighty-three, according to Ross, and Hope was prepared to give her a little bit of room given her age. She made sure she was at the correct number again, then pressed the doorbell.

Hope stood and waited but heard no movement from inside. Maybe the woman wasn't home, so Hope pressed the doorbell again. Again, she waited in vain as no one came to the door. Hope returned to the net curtain, this time peering intently inside. She could see an old woman sitting in a chair and the

TV was on. The image was fuzzy as she had to peer through the thick net curtains. But no, the woman was clearly awake. In fact, she just laughed at the TV. Hope knocked the window several times, but the woman didn't flinch. Hope knocked louder, thundering on the window frame. But again, the woman didn't move.

The door beside Annie's house opened and a woman stepped out. 'What are you doing,' she said, 'making that racket?'

Hope reached inside her leather jacket, pulling out her credentials. 'I'm DS Hope McGrath, and I'm looking to speak to an Annie Spence. I believe she's in that room there.'

'You don't think there's anything wrong with her?' asked the neighbour.

'No, I don't. She seems to be sitting, watching the television. She even laughed at it. She's not deaf, is she?'

'Only when she wants to be,' said the woman, laughing, and Hope was pushed aside as the woman approached the window, banging on it loudly and shouting, 'Annie, Annie, would you come to the blessed door.'

Hope smiled at the woman's effort, and the woman wasn't for backing down and she continued to bang, louder than what Hope had, until eventually she turned to Hope. 'Yes, she's coming.' Hope stood at the front door waiting until it was opened slightly.

'Yes?' came a voice from inside.

'I'm DS Hope McGrath. I'm here to interview you about The Cortado Club where I believe you go for coffee.'

'Yes?' came the reply.

Hope suddenly realised that the neighbour hadn't gone but was looking over her shoulder at that point. 'I'm sorry,' said Hope. 'Thank you for your help, but I really need to be interviewing Ms Stewart alone.'

'Oh, sorry. Yes, of course, you do, right. Well, if you need me at all, I'll just be next door.'

'Thank you, Mrs—'

'Mrs Macleod,' said the woman.

*Of course, it is. Has to be*, thought Hope. 'Mrs Stewart, I believe you're a frequenter of the coffee house, The Cortado Club. Is it okay if I ask you some questions?'

'You're awful young, aren't you, to be a detective? What did you say?'

'Detective Sergeant,' said Hope. 'And no, I'm not that young.'

'Where's the proper detective?'

Hope was momentarily taken aback. 'The proper detective?' said Hope. 'Who do you mean?'

'Macleod. Where is Macleod? I take it Macleod's here. We see Macleod on the television over in Inverness. I like Macleod. Is he here?'

'Detective Inspector Macleod is busy on the case. He sent me around to interview you.'

'Well, I want Macleod,' said the woman, 'and you're not coming in through this door until I get Macleod.'

'I'm sorry, but Detective Inspector Macleod won't be coming. I just want to know you were there yesterday when Donald MacDonald collapsed, weren't you?'

'Not without Macleod. You can ask the questions if you have to, but not without Macleod. I want to see Macleod.'

'Why?' asked Hope.

'I want the proper detective. I want that one, the one that's on the television, the one from here. I want the proper detective, Macleod. Now, where is Macleod?'

'I'm trying to tell you,' said Hope, 'Detective Inspector

Macleod will not be coming. It's me who's going to interview you. Okay?'

The door was shut in Hope's face. She banged on it. 'Mrs Stewart, you need to talk to me. I'm just going to ask you some simple questions. Would you open the door, please?'

There was no reply. Hope rapped on the door again. Looking to her left, she saw the neighbour had popped her head back out of the door. Obviously, the woman had never been far away.

'Have you got a problem?' the neighbour asked.

'She's not speaking. She says she wants Macleod.'

'Macleod? You can't want me?'

'No,' said Hope, 'My boss, Detective Inspector Macleod.'

'Oh, him from Inverness. He's from here, isn't he?'

'Yes, he is,' said Hope, 'but I can't get in here at the moment because she keeps saying she wants Macleod.'

'It's fine,' said Mrs Macleod, the neighbour. 'I'll sort it for you,' and she walked over to the window and started banging on it again.

'Listen, Annie, you need to talk. This is the police. This is Macleod's junior.'

*Macleod's junior*, thought Hope. *When have I ever been described as Macleod's junior?*

The woman continued to bang the window. 'Annie, you have to answer. You have to come and talk to her. Stop being ridiculous.'

Hope moved up beside the woman at the window and saw that the net curtains were pulled to one side. Annie was now standing in the window, looking down at the pair of them and she mouthed, 'Macleod. I want Macleod.'

The neighbour turned around to Hope again. 'She says she

wants Macleod.'

Hope stood, shaking her head. This was not the start to the day that she wanted. 'Look, thank you, Mrs—.' Hope's mind went blank.

'Macleod,' said the neighbour. 'Mrs Macleod. It's quite easy, isn't it? It's almost like everybody here is Macleod.'

*Well, not everybody*, thought Hope. 'Look, Mrs Macleod, thank you for your help. I'll come back later maybe with somebody from the island, a face she knows. That might be easier.'

'It might be, but I know Annie. If she wants Macleod, it'll be Macleod. Oh, she's getting set in her ways like that. That's just the way it is; don't take it personally, love. I'm sure you know how to do your detecting.'

'I'll do my best,' said Hope. 'Thanks again for your help.' Hope turned and walked off. Her next suspect to question was Sarah MacIver, and according to the staff at the coffee house, she would normally be up at the college in the castle grounds; the Highland and Islands University had one of its campuses based up in the castle grounds in Stornoway. Hope walked through town and across the bridge that linked the castle grounds to the harbour area of Stornoway. She then made a direct line, cutting through a forest, up past the golf course towards the college grounds, and saw a young girl making her way down.

'Excuse me,' said Hope. 'I don't suppose you know Sarah MacIver?'

'Who wants to know?' asked the young girl.

'Oh, sorry,' said Hope, putting out her credentials. 'I'm DS Hope McGrath. I'm just looking to speak to Sarah on a police matter.'

'A police matter? Well, you're talking to her,' said the girl.

Hope looked at a blonde-haired individual with blue eyes and a smile that could lift your soul. 'I need to ask you some questions,' said Hope, 'about The Cortado Club, the coffee house down in town.'

'I'm just on my way there,' said Sarah. 'It's about what happened yesterday with Donald?'

'Yes,' said Hope. 'Did you know Donald MacDonald?'

'Knew? Yes, to a point. He was always in the coffee house when I went down. I'm on my way there now. Why don't you walk down with me?'

Buoyed by this better turn of events after the cold shoulder she'd got from Annie Spence, Hope agreed, nodded, and started following Sarah back down through the castle grounds.

'So, you knew Donald MacDonald?' said Hope.

'Well, he was always there. You know how it is when you start to go to one of these establishments. You walk in, you see somebody, you might give a nod, say hello, but that was about it. I usually pop down, sit down with my laptop, do a couple of hours work, and then head back up to the college. It's just the way the timetable works. Most of my courses are in the afternoon. I have a couple in the morning, and then I've got the gap. Rather than stick up at the college, I prefer to come down and have a coffee. Almost like being away from everybody. Is that wrong?'

'I don't think so,' said Hope. 'Certainly not illegal. Did you also know Miranda well?'

'The other woman that died, not so well, 'she said. 'I knew her as Miranda. I didn't know the surname until it was in the paper that she'd died. I think Donald knew her quite well though. Well, at least I always got that feeling.'

79

'Why?' asked Hope.

'Well, they never spoke to each other, but they looked at each other. Do you know what I mean?'

'Could you elaborate a bit?' said Hope, but she did think she knew what the girl was saying.

'Well, right when you come in and you see him looking over and you think, oh, now, he obviously likes her, but then she's staring back. All the time back and forward, back and forward. I think that counsellor who used to sit beside Donald, I think he thought she was looking at him.'

'Really? Who was that?'

'He's a counsellor. Is it Morgan, I think? I don't know him either, but they used to sit together as a pair talking and laughing, but Donald got up and around the place, and that's why I knew it was him, because she would look at him when he was on the move away from Morgan.'

'Was there anybody else who used to come in at the same time as you?'

'Well, there's quite a number of us, isn't there, usually floating in at that time. There's the guy from the gun club. Innes, I think. Then there's the woman off the radio. I never listened to it. Joy. She runs the radio show *Filled with Joy* or something, isn't it? A bit much putting your own name in the title. I think Joy and Miranda knew each other, at least in some sort of way.'

'What do you mean?'

'Well, they used to come in and I felt they used to flirt a lot like they were after a man.'

'That's interesting, because I've been told Miranda tended to sit on her own.'

'Oh, always on her own,' said Sarah, 'but you saw what she wore at times. When you saw MacDonald, I think he liked what she wore. It was never ridiculous, but it was dressed to impress. I mean, I guess somebody of my age would find it a bit weird, but she'd be showing a bit of knee, her leg, long boots, stuff like that, even the occasional cleavage. Then Joy would come in and she'd be competing. I always thought it funny, for a church woman, some of the stuff she wore. Although nowadays, it's you-wear-what-you-want, isn't it?

'She seemed to have intent to it. I mean, it didn't bother me. They can wear whatever they want. It certainly affected Donald. The man had his tongue out half the time, and that Morgan guy. In fact, it was funny. Donald used to get very excited on seeing Miranda, and then when she left, he still seemed excited. Not been the same since though, he seemed quite down and narky since she passed on. Maybe he really did like her. I don't know.'

Hope realised that they'd come to the door of the coffee house and she held it open with her hand, allowing Sarah inside.

'This is normally when I get down. I'm regular as clockwork because the timing's up to the college. Is there anything else you want to know?'

'Just about yourself, Sarah,' said Hope, as they reached the counter. Sarah turned and ordered a coffee, but Hope put her hand up and Sarah offered her one.

'I can't be doing that,' she said, 'people read things into a kind gesture.'

'Okay, suit yourself,' said Sarah, and went and found an empty table and sat down. Hope pulled up a seat beside her.

'What would you say if I told you that Donald and Miranda were both poisoned?'

'I find it quite weird,' she said,' because the food in this place is fine and coffee, I've never heard anybody going off with a bad coffee. Maybe the milk would go off, but that wouldn't kill you, would it?'

'I'm not talking about that,' said Hope. 'It looks like they both may have been poisoned.'

The young girl looked at her. 'You're trying to tell me that somebody killed them?'

'Indeed,' said Hope. 'I was just wondering, but do you know of any reason somebody would have to kill them? Did you have any knowledge of anything they did that was wrong or against anyone's beliefs?'

'Me?' said Sarah. 'I told you, I barely knew them. I'm a people watcher. I come in here, I look, I watch. I think Miranda was as well. She did that. She looked over at Donald a lot, but she also could watch everyone else coming.'

'Do you have any one reason why anyone would want to harm you?' asked Hope.

'Why do you ask me that?' she said.

'It's just a long shot. After all, you come down here the same time as they did. I'm wondering, does anyone here know about it?'

'Well, Donald died here, but Miranda didn't, did she?'

'No, she didn't,' said Hope. 'She died at home, but they were both poisoned. Look, I can't give you much more detail than that, but do you know of anyone who would be seeking your demise?'

'Not that I know of. I owe my father a fortune for doing this course, but other than that, no. I keep myself to myself, I don't go out a lot in the evenings, working away at my course.'

'When you come and sit here, do you ever get up?'

'What do you mean?' asked Sarah.

'Do you ever get up? You say you people watch; you said Donald got up and about. Do you ever get up and talk to people?'

'No,' said Sarah, 'I sit here, I watch. If they say hello, I say hello back. That's it. The furthest I've been on my feet in here is over to the toilet. Outside of that, I don't get up. You can ask anyone. Oh, I might get back up if I want a second coffee, but that will be it.'

'Okay,' said Hope. 'Thank you for that. Don't go anywhere, I might need to talk to you again.'

'Well, you know where to catch me. Five days a week, I'm up at the college. I'm sure you'll find an address for me.'

'Just give me that,' said Hope, taking out her notepad. As she wrote down the address Sarah gave to her, she saw Clarissa enter the café with a man.

# Chapter 10

Clarissa left the Cortado Club and made her way back to the station to talk to Ross. Between him and Sergeant Dolan, she had managed to get a contact number for Innes Stewart. On a quick call to his house, she found that he was out at the gun range in Harris, the island just to the south of Lewis. The pair were connected and Clarissa thought it was a good chance to meet him away from everyone, to see him in his normal abode.

She jumped into the car, took the road out of Stornoway that headed south to Harris, and watched as the moorland passed by on either side. The road was not straight, but rather skipped here and there showing many an impressive loch before passing through the town of Balallan and out further towards Harris. She could see the Clisham in the distance, the island's largest mountain but she stopped short of it, turning into a wooded area.

There was a large gate across a road with a sign the Harris Gun Club had put up in front of it. She stepped out, opened the gate, and decided to walk in. Clarissa was dressed in a large shawl, this one green. As a nod to the team, she was currently wearing a smart pair of denim jeans with thick leather boots on her feet.

Her purple hair began to blow as she broke the cover of the trees. She looked around, saw an expanse in front of her, which seemed to fall away. When turning to her right, she saw a number of huts, and ahead of her were other huts and she began to realise where she was. There was a mechanical arm which swung and two discs came flying out well in front of her. There were two cracks from a shotgun and both discs exploded. Clarissa turned and saw the smoke emanating from the hut to her right and she began to make her way towards it, making sure she stayed behind the hut at all times.

When she arrived, she saw it had a backdoor entrance and she knocked on it just as two more shots were fired off. The door opened and one open shotgun was in the arms of a blond-haired man looking back at her. He could only be twenty-five. Clarissa thought if she was twenty years younger, the man might've had a chance. As it was, she decided she had probably drawn the best straw out of the hat.

'I'm looking for an Innes Stewart?' said Clarissa.

'That's me,' said the man. 'Who are you?'

Clarissa reached inside her shawl and pulled out her credentials. 'Clarissa Urquhart. I'm over from Inverness. We're investigating some deaths in Stornoway. You may have heard yesterday, Donald MacDonald has died.'

'Heard? I was there,' said Innes, 'you were there as well. Do you not remember my face? You might not, I was kind of a bit back. Annie went over to you; she was harassing you.'

'The old woman,' said Clarissa. 'Yes, I remember her.'

'Troubled soul,' said the man. 'Do you need me to stop? It's just I'm in the middle of practice.'

'I saw,' said Clarissa, 'not a bad shot.'

'Island Games winner. Trying to get good enough to get into the UK squad. Have you ever shot?'

'I'm not bad,' said Clarissa. 'it's been a while though.'

'Where did you shoot?'

'Was brought up on a farm. Well, an estate actually. We didn't shoot those things though; we shot the real thing. Sent the dogs out to get them.'

'Frowned on these days, isn't it, by a lot of people? I don't mind shooting these things. I do it for fun. I'm not looking to keep any game or run hunting parties. Why don't you have a go? I'll get a gun out for you.'

Clarissa thought for a moment. Macleod would probably frown upon the experience, but what the hey—he wasn't here. She could have a couple of clay pigeons with this young man.

'Go on, then,' said Clarissa. Making her way over, she took a shotgun off the man and some ammunition, placing it on a table inside the hut.

'How well did you know Donald MacDonald?'

'Well, you know faces, don't you? I got to know them. I knew he was Donald. I think I'd heard the MacDonald occasionally. Are you okay with that gun though? You know what you're doing?'

Clarissa loaded the shotgun, cocked it, put it up, looking down the sight. 'I'm fine with the gun,' she said. 'Now, why were you in the Cortado Club?'

'I like coffee,' said the man. 'Ready?'

'Pull,' said Clarissa. Two disks flew out and she took aim firing once and then twice. She put the shotgun down in front of her.

'You have shot before,' said the man, 'haven't you?'

'Yes, I have,' said Clarissa. 'Now would you tell me, why do

86

you go to the Cortado Club? You live here, in Harris. I've just driven out here; it's quite a drive, so why bother going there?'

'The coffee—because I like the coffee; it's enjoyable. You find it hard to get a cuppa like that down here. The more you move away from Stornoway, the more everything gets a little bit more rough and ready.'

Clarissa wasn't sure quite how his fellow locals would take that, but she decided that wasn't her problem. 'But from what I've heard, you're down every day. That's quite something, to go all that way every day just for a coffee.'

'Well, my job's a ranger,' he said. 'I can do most of that towards the morning. I get to organise my own time. I do some of it at night when I come back. It just gives a routine to my day. As I say, it's what I like. I wasn't born and bred out in the sticks. I grew up in a city and then came back here when I was about fifteen. My parents are from the island, and they probably thought I'd leave it again, but I got this job which suits me down to the ground because, to be honest, there's not a lot of work in what I do, although I don't tell anybody that. I also then got good with a shotgun, got into these Island Games. The standard is not Olympic standard, but hey, it's better than anything I ever did.'

The man pressed the button, two discs flew out across the skyline and then exploded as the shotgun was fired twice.

'Well, you can certainly shoot,' said Clarissa and began reloading her gun, 'but let me get this right,' said Clarissa. 'You come up here, you do a bit of shooting then you head into town. You're in town nearly the same time every day because they told me that down at the café, and then what do you do in town? Have a coffee and go back?'

'No, I usually have something to do so I'm usually kicking

about until at least five or six.'

'Okay, and then at five or six, what do you do?'

'Usually back up the road, this direction. In my house anything from seven onwards, seven or eight.'

'Right,' said Clarissa, 'so you're down in town until about five or six, then your back up here, road. You're in your house by seven or eight. Is it seven or is it eight?'

'The truth, I guess, if you asked my folks, it would be 8:00.'

'So, you still live with them?' said Clarissa.

'Yes. How did you know I was here?'

'Well, I spoke to a woman in the house but I didn't fully understand who it was. I thought it might just be somebody you live with.'

'No, that's my mother,' said Innes. 'Do you want one more?'

'Go on,' said Clarissa. She cocked her gun, holding it up, and shouted, 'Pull.' Two discs flew across the sky, and she shot the first one but the second one, she just let go.

'You didn't take a shot at that one.'

'No,' said Clarissa, 'but I will do, and I'll take a shot at you if you don't start telling me the truth.'

'I don't know what you mean,' he said and pressed the button raising his shotgun up and taking two clay pigeons out of the air.

'Thanks for the shoot,' said Clarissa. 'I guess you'll be making your way into town now.'

'Yes.'

'Why don't I drive you in?' said Clarissa. 'I could drive you back again tonight when you're done. It's not a problem for me, my boss wants me to find out information about people who were in the Cortado Club so I can drive you there and back.'

'You could drive me down. I'll get the bus back,' he said.

'Okay, what are you doing in town this afternoon?'

'I've got a few things to pick up before coming back. They're light enough, I'll take them on the bus. Okay?'

'For work or for the house, your parents?'

'For work,' he said. 'It's usually work stuff I need to pick up.'

Clarissa nodded and let the man lock up as he put the guns and the ammunition away. She noticed they were stored in two separate places and when the man made it inside to her car, she could see he was beginning to get a little bit agitated.

'You'll be down for your coffee soon,' she said. 'That'll be enjoyable, won't it? What do you normally drink?'

'Cortado,' he said.

'I should have known,' said Clarissa. 'I need to start talking to you about the people there. Did you know Donald MacDonald that well?'

'No, I told you. He's just a face that I got to know.'

'What about Miranda? Miranda Folly?'

'The woman that died?' he said.

'Yes, the woman that died; what about her?'

'No, I didn't know her that well. She stayed in the corner all the time. She didn't really speak to anyone, always looking around though, especially following that Donald guy. I don't know but I thought they knew each other.'

'What, like in a romantic fashion?' said Clarissa.

'No, no, I wouldn't say that. Well, not that I knew. Just they always seem to be looking towards each other. To be honest, I wasn't that bothered. I'd go in, sit down, usually read a paper, pick up my lunch.'

'You're not put off then by the talk of poisonings coming out of that shop?'

'Food poisoning? You don't get food poisoning from coffee. I've seen their sandwiches being brought in and made. You're not going to get food poisoning off that. They're kept in the fridge; they're gone within an hour or two. Even the cake is not there for more than a day or two. It's a load of nonsense. That's the trouble with this place. Things get whipped up and out of proportion. Happens a lot.'

'Who else is usually in around that time?'

'I don't know what you call her but she's a blonde girl. I think she comes down from the college or that. She's in every day with her laptop. I know because she always gives me a smile. Not interested though.'

'No? A young man like yourself?' said Clarissa. 'Why not? Intelligent woman if she's up at the college.'

'No, I'm quite happy. Very happy being single.'

Clarissa looked across and the man's eyes were cast down looking into the well of the car.

'I've got a problem,' said Clarissa.

'What do you mean?' asked Innes.

'It isn't just shooting I've done in the past; I've done a lot of things. I'm very good at telling when a person lies to me and you're lying to me at the moment. The thing is, I think it's for a good reason. I think you're trying to protect someone or some aspect of your life. You need to tell me because if you don't, we're going to have to go and find out and dig it up in a proper way. Now, if we dig it up in a proper way, it goes on record and suddenly the wrong people get to know.'

'What are you talking about?'

'Well, it'll get into the local police force. Sometimes somebody in there knows somebody's mother or father and they let go that such and such happened because they don't think

90

it's particularly important. Of course, they shouldn't do that, but I've seen it happen.'

'What are you trying to say?'

'Okay,' said Clarissa as she turned the corner. 'Cards on the table. Five o'clock to eight o'clock, who were you with?'

'I told you. I travel back from town.'

'Yes, with who? Where do you go during that bit in the middle?'

'I don't know what you mean,' the man said.

'When I was in the gun club you handed me a separate shotgun, but I looked around, and do you know what I saw?'

'No,' he said.

'Two bottles sitting together, two packets of crisps, then there was two of something else. All the waste was two. Not only that, but it also wasn't just two of everything, albeit slightly different. There was a bottle of this, a bottle of that but two together. Everything was together. It wasn't one bit over here, one over there, fairly tidy though so most of that must have been recent. You hadn't moved it; you haven't been complaining about it by the looks of it because you'd probably know nobody is coming today. Therefore, you can clear it up tonight when you're back there.'

The man's face went red. 'Look,' he said, 'you can't tell them. You can't let them know.'

'Let who know what?' asked Clarissa. 'If it's innocent and it's nothing to do with the case, I won't tell anyone, I might not even tell my boss. He certainly won't tell anyone if it's got nothing to do with the other bad business. I need you to tell me, Innes, who do you go with? Who are you bringing back?'

The man looked out the window then looked back at Clarissa. 'Amy,' he said.

'Okay, and who's Amy? Please don't tell me she's a fifteen-year-old from the school.'

'No,' he said, 'of course, she isn't. She's from Stornoway but she's not from the island originally. She's a bit different. I don't think my father and mother would take to her.'

'Why?' asked Clarissa.

'Well, she kind of stands out.'

'What? Is she a goth or something?'

'No,' he said. 'She's black. We don't have that many black people up here, we have a few and we have some Indians, and my father and mother are quite happy to let them come up and live here, but if I went back with her and said we were an item . . .'

'Yes, I get you,' said Clarissa. 'Can I get you to do something for me?'

'What?' the man asked.

'Get Amy to ring this phone number and I'll speak to her tonight. I'll meet her and collaborate that, and then that's it. She also could be a good alibi for you.'

'Alibi?' he said. 'Do I need an alibi?'

'We have two people who have been poisoned. Understand this, Innes, they were poisoned. It wasn't food poisoning, and it wasn't an accident. They were poisoned.'

The man stared ahead. 'Why?'

'That's what we're trying to find out,' said Clarissa. 'Let's go have a coffee.'

# Chapter 11

Macleod walked from the police station towards the war memorial set up high on a hill above Stornoway. He remembered in his youth looking up there, seeing it often like a beacon, even more so than Lews Castle. When he was very young, he wondered what it was. Not long after that, he would see the men on Remembrance Day heading up the path. When he was old enough, he was there as well. It had ingrained in him a thought to remember them for the rest of his life.

Quite often, the focus on the island was regarding the *Iolaire*, a ship that had gone down at the end of World War I, taking with it many returning soldiers. He was never quite sure what happened on that boat. He'd been told again and again about the struggle to get the short distance from the boat to land and the treacherous sea and rocks between the sailors and safety. Whenever he thought of that incident, he remembered that in joyous times, the next tragedy wasn't far around the corner. It was a morbid outlook, and one he was slowly ridding himself of, learning instead to use it as a reminder to enjoy the good times.

The other difficulty with the *Iolaire* tragedy was it happened literally around the corner from where his wife died, entering the water as a suicide, just off Holm. While he was more at peace with what she did, it still cut a raw nerve whenever it was brought up.

The memorial sat high on the hill behind an estate. It was up the street that led to the War Memorial that Macleod climbed before reaching the house of Joy Grundy. The outside of the property had a number of trees shielding it from the street and making the door hard to see. Macleod located a small gate that led to a path across a garden to the front of the house. As he went to rap on the large knocker, the door opened, and he was greeted by a brunette woman who at first smiled at him before looking slightly quizzical.

'You don't have the delivery then?'

Macleod thought about what he was wearing. A long raincoat, shirt and tie, black trousers and shoes. *Who delivers to this house normally?*

'No, I'm afraid I'm not the delivery service, ma'am. My name's Detective Inspector Seoras Macleod and I'm here to talk to you about the recent death of Donald MacDonald.'

'Oh,' said the woman, 'Donald; tragic. Saw it right before my very eyes. Tubes was quite a man. She'll miss him. I'll tell you that for nothing, Inspector. She'll miss him.'

'If it's possible, I'd like to come inside and talk about this,' said Macleod.

'Well, it's really a bad time, Inspector. I need to get off for a meeting. Actually, I'm meeting down at the Cortado club. You're welcome to walk with me and talk if you wish, but I really can't back out of this one. Treasurer you see, the local women's guild. I need to make sure the accounts are up to date. To be honest, there's a few things I need to ask questions

94

about.'

'All right, anything I should know about?' asked Macleod.

Joy Grundy laughed. 'Of course not, no, of course not,' she said. 'Just a moment and I'll be right with you.'

Macleod watched the woman turn and she picked up a yellow rain jacket off a hook in the hallway, put it on, and zipped it up the front. Underneath, she wore blouse and trousers, and on her feet were ankle-length boots. Macleod wouldn't have said she was a sex symbol but certainly, she had a personality that took hold of you. He understood the type of man that would be very engaged with Joy, even if she seemed too full on for himself. Then, he thought of his own Jane. Maybe he'd need to rethink that comment.

'This way, Inspector, come on. I can't be late for the meeting.'

'I'll do the best I can to keep up. I feel I've got a few years on you.'

'Nonsense. You look splendid, Inspector. Now, what is it you want to know?'

'Did you know Donald MacDonald well?' asked Macleod.

'Oh, Donald. Well, I've known him really since school days. We weren't that far apart in years, and he was always quite the catch. I remember when he went to get married, a lot of girls were distraught at that one. Never quite sure how Donella managed to grab him. She was a quiet soul, very under the radar, Inspector, if you know what I mean?'

Macleod nodded as he understood he wasn't going to get a word in edgeways.

'The thing with Donella was, she was probably a perfect wife. She was quiet, she went to the church, good standing, and reputation. She wasn't going to go on and make a lot of herself, so she'd be at home for the kids. That's what a lot of the island men wanted back then.'

'And you're not like that,' said Macleod.

'Oh, no. Oh, no. I've always wanted to be something, do something, you know? Too lively for most of them. That's my trouble. That's why I'm still single.'

'Never been married?' asked Macleod.

'No,' said Joy, 'never. That doesn't mean I haven't had my fair share of encounters, but no; what about yourself, Inspector?'

'You probably remember,' said Macleod.

'Oh, right. Of course, I would've been in my teens. Your wife, she . . .'

'She committed suicide at Holm,' said Macleod looking directly at the woman trying to gauge a response.

'Tragic, must have been hard. You moved away after that, didn't you?'

'Yes, I did,' said Macleod.

The woman leaned over to him, putting an arm around him. 'Can't be easy. Was she a love to you or just a wife?'

'She was one of the two best women I've ever met,' said Macleod, 'and I probably didn't know it at the time.'

Joy stopped, turned around, and put her arms around Macleod, pulling him close. Macleod made no effort to engage her, but he felt like she was an unstoppable force. She then sprung back off him, smiling broadly.

'Forgive me, inspector, if I'm too forward. I just felt you needed that. These things can be hard, and you should really take some compassion in the arms of another. I know other men I've engaged with have found that.'

'If I'm not mistaken, you're quite high up in the church,' said Macleod, almost as a rebuke.

'That I am,' she said, 'and alas, a lot of the ones at the top of that church you wouldn't touch with a barge pole. I like a man with a bit of fight in him. Either that or a bit of quiet, dogged, determination, Inspector.'

Macleod nodded but didn't take the bait. 'Was Donald MacDonald like that?' he asked.

'Donald was super friendly,' said Joy, 'I had a lot of time for him.'

'You'd see him most days I take it,' said Macleod.

'I don't know why you think that, Inspector, but yes, it's true. I'm a big fan of the Cortado club. I'm down there most days, but not to see Donald. I'm usually there for meetings like I am today or one or two of the other girls to chat to. Then, I've got the radio show on a Sunday. Have you ever listened to it?'

'We don't tend to get it in Inverness,' said Macleod, 'and I'm not one for music radio. I prefer chat.'

'Oh, you might like my show then, Inspector. In fact, to have you on would be great. It's quite intimate, lets people express deeper views. We talk about tragedy and about how people are helped to get through things. Maybe you'd like to come on and talk about your past.'

'If I was to talk about my past,' said Macleod, 'I'd have to talk about my present.'

'How so?'

'My current partner, Jane, she's one of the ones who's helped me through this. She's quite bubbly, lively woman, bit like yourself. Second-best woman I found in life, although, I don't know anymore which I would choose. It was a different age back then and I'm older now. Jane's more teasing. Whereas Hope, Hope was more . . .'

'Like a soulmate, gently teasing you into things that you didn't really do because you were so staid.'

Macleod looked up at Joy Grundy and decided he'd have to watch her carefully. The woman had an ability to pick up the undercurrent of what was being said.

'Yes.'

'Well,' said Joy, 'I think you need the bubbly and lively now; it's what I tell most men.'

'You're not behind the door, are you, Miss Grundy?'

'People who are behind the door don't see what's ahead of them, don't open the door, and don't find out what God has in life for them. I feel you found what he had for you, inspector.'

'That's true, but if you don't mind, can we talk a little bit less about me and more about you? Otherwise, those who pay my bills may have some questions.'

'Of course, Inspector. Sorry, I just took a moment. I felt you needed it.'

Macleod gave a cough, and then as they continued walking, decided to see what Joy knew about Miranda Folly.

'Donald's not been the only death though. Miranda Folly died as well, and I have it on good authority that she was down at the club usually around the same time as Donald and possibly yourself.'

'Miranda Folly,' said Joy, her tone becoming slightly darker. 'Now there was a strange one. She was quite the enticer.'

'There's nothing wrong with being enticing,' said Macleod.

'But in what way, Inspector? She liked to dress in a way that got hold of a man, not to show her vivacious side. It was darker. More carnal, less loving.'

'You know this for a fact?' said Macleod.

'Donald, God rest his soul, he was enticed by her, very much so. I used to try and talk to him so he wouldn't be near her, but he kept looking at her.'

98

'There's nothing illegal about looking at someone.'

'There is when you look like that, Inspector. It might not be illegal, but it's against what he signed up for.'

'Meaning?' asked Macleod.

'He chose Donella. Even I had to accept that. Sure, I could flirt with Donald, I could have a laugh, but he chose Donella, and I would never break that.'

'That's not entirely what I've heard,' said Macleod.

'Oh,' said Joy, not in the faintest embarrassed. 'What have you heard?'

'Well, the owner said that you were quite engaged with Donald. I heard that you used to come in dressed to grab the eye, as you would probably say.'

'Well, Inspector, that's probably true on the odd occasion. It's not easy when you go through life on your own. I'm sure you understand that. Sometimes I would try and grab his eye, never with the intention to take him away. Sometimes it's good to be appreciated. Did you ever miss that?'

'You're trying to talk about me again,' said Macleod. 'I specifically asked to talk about you. What were your feelings towards Miranda Folly then? Did you hate her?'

'You don't hate, Inspector. The good Lord taught us not to hate.'

'The good Lord teaches a lot of people in the churches in this island a lot of things, and I'll tell you now that when my wife walked into the sea, they hated her. They hated her, and they dumped most of that anger towards me. Forgive me if I don't just stand here and take that as accepted that you would follow that rule. Now, what did you think truly of Miranda Folly?'

Joy Grundy stopped. Macleod realised they were only a

99

hundred yards from the coffee house.

'Did you know she wrote novels, Inspector?'

'Yes,' said Macleod, 'I'm well aware of what she wrote.'

'Don't get me wrong, inspector. I like a flirt. I like a bit of fun and games, but what she was writing, it's dark.'

'For dark, some people would substitute intense,' said Macleod, even though he wouldn't have put that word in.

'You shouldn't mess around with things that are on the dark side,' said Joy. 'Takes people down.'

'Did she take Donald down?' asked Macleod.

'I don't know,' said Joy, 'I don't truly know. I suspect she did.'

'Donella says he used to go to the coffee house for two hours every day and at least occasionally longer.'

'It wasn't two hours, Inspector, forty minutes to an hour, tops. That was Donald and he was out of there. Funny enough, Miranda was out of there too. I did notice.'

'And you did what?'

'I tried to save him,' said Joy, 'from himself.'

They started to walk towards the coffee shop again where Macleod held the door open, allowing Joy to enter.

'A chivalrous man as well. You really are quite the mystery, Macleod.'

'There's no mystery about me, and I'm not the one to be solved,' he said. 'Please take a seat.'

'Can I get you a coffee though, Inspector?' asked Joy.

'No,' said Macleod. 'If you understand the business, I'll pay for it. Not good to have a suspect being owed something.'

'A suspect am I,' said Joy. 'What makes you think I'm a suspect?'

'You told me you're an intense woman. You told me you like to flirt. Your mannerism towards me quite frankly says to me that you're lonely. I appreciate that. It's not a crime. You tell me you tried to save Donald and maybe you couldn't, and now I've got two dead bodies.'

Macleod approached the counter. When he turned back, Joy Grundy had taken off her yellow jacket, sitting at a table, and had positioned a chair beside her for Macleod. He shimmied over, placed two Cortados on the table, and didn't take off his coat as he sat down.

'I won't bite,' said Joy. 'You can take the coat off.'

The woman was overbearing almost, and yet he had to admit, in a pleasant way. Her face was kind, and yet he found himself constantly wanting space away from her, to walk away from this interview. Yet he knew if he was single, he'd be enticed, fighting the urge to move because the woman really was quite engaging, and more worryingly for Macleod, she seemed earnest and sincere.

'How much did you really love Donald?'

'Honestly, Inspector, Donella should never have got hold of him. He should have taken a risk. Sounds to me like you did, and I know you paid for it. Sounds like it was worth it. Maybe you should have got away from here earlier. Maybe then, it would've worked out better.'

'Maybe I should have,' said Macleod, 'but once again, it's not about me. I have a murderer on the loose. I have two people dead, so if you'll forgive me, let's talk some more.'

101

# Chapter 12

Macleod continued to talk to Joy Grundy for the next ten minutes. During that time, he found her chair moving closer to him, and several times, her knee touched his. When he looked up, as if to say that was enough, she simply smiled at him in a way that was reminiscent of Jane.

'If you reckoned that Donald was having an affair with Miranda Folly, why didn't you say anything to Donella? I take it you don't have anything against the woman. Donella, I mean.'

'Donella is a friend, not a close one. Church friend, maybe, you would call it if you understand my drift. But she's got a large family, and I had no proof, Inspector. I had proof enough for me, I could tell, but I'm sure in your job, you're aware that proof needs to be a bit more than that. You look like a man who solves a murder before you produce the proof.'

Macleod was feeling uncomfortable with how well this woman was reading him. As he looked away, he noted that Annie Spence had entered the coffee house, and made her way over to a corner seat on her own. As Joy continued to talk, Macleod saw a Cortado arrive for Annie, and she sipped it slowly.

'Did you warn Donald directly?' asked Macleod. 'Did you ever follow him?'

'I didn't need to follow him; he was off to Miranda's. She lives in the backend of nowhere, it's perfect. Disappear off there for an hour, do whatever. I wouldn't be surprised if she had some sort of dungeon in the bottom, the stuff that she writes.'

'Have you read much of it?' asked Macleod.

'It's not my cup of tea,' said Joy. Macleod realised she had read a lot of it. 'I like a romantic novel, Inspector. I don't mind a bit of physicality in it; that's all part of the fun, isn't it? But it needs to be wholesome with regards to the people.'

'Do you know how many novels she has written?' asked Macleod.

'Over forty, from what I've heard.'

'Heard or looked up?'

Joy Grundy laughed. 'You're good, Inspector. You're very good.'

'Kindle, did you read it on a Kindle? I bet you read those ones on a Kindle,' said Macleod. 'They won't be in paperback. They could be found lying around the house. Kindles are good. You can read whatever you want, store it away, as long as somebody doesn't pick it up by accident. Even then, I think, can you lock those ones out? Put a screen password in. Put those books in a separate entry maybe. Ross, my constable, he can do all sorts of things with computers. I don't think you're on his level, but unlike me, you probably know what you're doing.'

Joy simply smiled and then turned to engage a woman who arrived through the door. There was a brief moment of chatter, and then Joy turned back to Macleod, moving her chair even closer so that the whole of her thigh was now touching his leg.

'You're in luck, inspector. They've cancelled the meeting. I'm not going anywhere else, so we can talk longer.'

'I don't think there's much more to say.'

'In that case, why don't we talk about you? Tell me a bit more about yourself, Inspector. When you first met Jane, what attracted you to her? What is it you look for in a woman?' Joy Grundy's hand was now moving towards Macleod, and he spotted it from a mile away. His eyes shot up, and he saw Councillor Morgan coming in through the door, and so Macleod stood up abruptly.

'Apologies, Miss Grundy, it appears my second interviewee has just arrived. I'm going to have to go and speak to him. It's been an absolute pleasure.'

'Anytime, Inspector. Why don't you come and do the radio show? You can come around to mine first of all, for a spot of dinner or maybe it's better to have the dinner afterwards.'

'It's probably better that a serving inspector doesn't go on such an intimate show, especially to talk about the death of someone. But thank you for the offer,' said Macleod, and turned away.

Councillor Morgan had taken a seat in the far corner of the coffee house, and Macleod picked up his Cortado and approached. He sat down opposite him, and Morgan looked suspiciously towards him.

'Sorry to disturb you, Councillor; my name is Detective Inspector Macleod.' Reaching inside his coat, Macleod pulled out his credentials and flashed them at the councillor. 'I'm here to talk about your friend, Donald MacDonald.'

'Terrible business,' said Morgan. 'Terrible business, but

I heard you're not looking to see whose shop isn't up to standard.'

'Indeed, I'm not,' said Macleod. 'Word gets out fast, doesn't it?'

'Well, being a councillor, I do have my contacts.'

'I heard that Donald was your friend.'

'A firm friend, all through life. Terrible, terrible for Donella and the kids. Such a guy, really good guy.'

'Donella told me,' said Macleod, 'that he used to come down here every day for his coffee.'

'Yes, like a routine thing, we'd meet up. Didn't always talk to me, he liked getting the buzz of the room, walking about, talking to whoever. It's a good thing. As a councillor, I have to do it as well. Keep yourself out there.'

'But Donald didn't, did he? Have to keep himself out there. His work was a bit different. I heard he was into finance and helping people with money.'

'That's true, Inspector, but really he just wanted to get on with people. Great man.'

'How long did he spend down here when he was with you?'

'Oh,' said Morgan, 'an hour at the most. Come in, have his coffee, have a wander and a chat. Then he was off.'

'That's interesting because Donella used to say he was down here for at least two hours, sometimes longer. Do you know where he went after that?'

Councillor Morgan became a little bit awkward. 'Well, a man's business is his own, isn't it?'

'I didn't ask that. I asked if you know where he went—yes or no?' reiterated Macleod. 'The man is dead.'

'I had a good idea.'

'And that idea is what?'

105

Morgan looked around him, leaned over, and in a hushed whisper, said, 'Probably off to Miranda Folly's. He had a thing for her. Don't really blame him. He had her, he had that Joy Grundy, both of them almost fighting for him. That would be nice, don't you think, Inspector?'

'I don't think much about how I would feel,' said Macleod. 'I think about how he feels, and more importantly, about how other people felt about that. Were you jealous at all?'

'No. No, of course not.'

'I gather Miss Folly was a bit of an exciting woman,' said Macleod, 'if you get my drift.'

'Racy is the word you're looking for. Although, I don't know if that's an image she cultivated. Maybe she was just lonely,' said Morgan.

'Well, that's a different take. Why do you say that?' asked Macleod.

'Well, we never got that side of things; only people who read her novels. Maybe she's just writing it. Maybe she's just saying these things writing out a fantasy. Maybe when you get down to it, she's quite an ordinary person, usual desires and that. I mean, I'm not saying that they were innocent together, but I doubt it was like her books.'

'You read many of them?' asked Macleod.

'Oh, yes,' said Morgan. 'Of course, I don't admit that to anyone.'

'Does the wife know?'

'It was the wife that read them first,' said Morgan. 'Of course, it took us a while to work out that they were actually her books.'

'How did you know?'

'Well, Donald mentioned it one day. I tried to ask him how he found out, but he wouldn't tell me.'

Macleod saw this as almost a conclusion. There was an affair; there had to be.

'You suspected he had an affair then,' said Macleod quietly.

'I think it's more than suspect.'

'Do you have any proof?'

'You would call it circumstantial, Inspector. It's probably much like you think, disappeared off, always two or three minutes after Miranda disappeared out the door. He certainly looked at her and she looked at him in between, Joy Grundy trying to barge her way in. To be honest, I felt a bit jealous about it. I really did. I thought I had more going for me than Donald did. Didn't understand why I didn't get a look. Damn, inspector, I looked at her often enough.'

'You mean Miranda.'

'Miranda, Joy. I'm in one of those more sedate marriages, shall we say. She's a good woman, but she's lost that edge. She's not interested in that side. I hear it's all too common, but I don't know.'

Macleod didn't know either. He felt a moment of sympathy for the man.

'You don't feel like you were hard done by, that you should have been there.'

'No, no. It's just my mind going for a wander, isn't it? Like it does. I'm sure you can understand that, Inspector. I never followed them, I never checked out what they were doing, I never tried to intervene. All my thoughts were simply in my head. It was quite clear she was interested in Donald. In fact, they both were. Although, I don't know where Donella would have stood with that.'

'Did you ever feel you should tell her?'

'Well, to be honest,' said Morgan, 'I always thought that I

would if I had proper proof, if I knew for definite.'

'You could have followed them,' said Macleod.

'I could, but then I would've had proper proof. I know, Inspector, I'm a coward, but he was my friend; so was Donella. It would've been a mess.'

Macleod looked at the man. Morgan was hanging his head in shame and Macleod thought this was a good moment to make a move for the bathroom, something he'd wanted to do since he'd arrived. He'd been bursting but had to wait due to the investigation he was running. He excused himself from Morgan.

As he stood up, he saw Hope enter with Sarah MacIver, both taking up a seat. Making his way across the room, he went through a door to a cloak room to then enter the bathroom beyond. He was feeling a little bit derailed by the attention of Joy Grundy. Macleod took a while to sit down and think through what had been happening. When he finally exited the bathroom, he saw that Councillor Morgan had departed. He also noticed that during the time of his absence in the bathroom, Clarissa had arrived within Innes Stewart.

He walked over to his sergeant to advise that he would be departing back to the station. Clarissa said she would follow shortly. After a moment, he gave Hope the same message and made his way out onto the street. As he departed the café, he felt he was being followed and turned around to see Joy Grundy in a yellow raincoat standing behind him.

'That's somewhat spooky,' said Macleod.

'You knew I was behind you, didn't you?' said Joy. 'I think there's a link between us, don't you?

'I think there might be a link between you in what's going on,' said Macleod, hoping to catch the woman off guard, but instead, she simply smiled.

'I'm sure if you got to know me better, it would be very clear that I wouldn't be doing anything like that.'

'Miss Grundy, I hope this isn't out of line, but even if it is, I'm going to say it anyway. I'm a Detective Inspector. You're a suspect. I'm also a man with a partner.'

'Not married then,' said Joy.

'As good as,' said Macleod. 'While I won't say that I find your intentions repugnant or that I find you displeasing. I will say this. I am not interested. To pursue anything anyway at this time, would be highly incorrect when I'm taking part in an investigation. Do you understand me?'

'I understand you perfectly, Inspector. It's part of what makes you so attractive, an upright man. They all like you on the team, I bet they do. You've got that firmness. You stand up and can be all macho.'

Macleod nearly burst out laughing inside. The last thing he ever thought of himself as was macho.

'You're also silent and deep,' said Joy. 'I think you'd be a ton of fun, Inspector. A ton of fun to be with.'

'Well, I can advise you that I am a ton of fun to be with,' said Macleod. 'Yes, my partner says so. I think she's off her rocker. As long as she stays off it, that's fine by me, but be very, very sure that she's the only one I want to be with at the moment. Now, if you'd kindly leave me alone, I have a murder to solve.'

Macleod strode up towards the station. Climbing up a short hill and then walking along the street behind the harbour, he saw the back of a hotel and the Masonic lodge. Then as he was making his way into the rear entrance of the police station, his phone rang. It was Ross.

'Inspector, Ross here. A call's just come through.'

'What is it, Ross?'

'Councillor Morgan, sir. He's just collapsed. I think he's in the back of an ambulance at the moment heading for the hospital.'

'Where are you, Ross?'

'At the station, sir.'

'Get into the car park. Grab the car. I'll meet you there.'

Macleod ran into the car park and had to wait about twenty seconds until Ross came running out with the keys. With the car open, they jumped inside and tore off out of the station down towards the harbourfront and along up towards the hospital. As he came onto the harbourfront, Macleod saw Joy Grundy in her raincoat looking across the street. She smiled at him. That made him wonder just quite what the intent of it was.

Councillor Morgan was now fighting for his life. Joy Grundy had seen him, talked to Morgan. She'd almost been teasing Macleod and she certainly told him that Donald MacDonald had been a target of her affection, but Miranda Folly had taken him away. *What lay behind the eyes of the woman? What lay behind that fun and engaging exterior?* Macleod sat back in the car, his mind pondering as Ross raced through the traffic towards the hospital.

# Chapter 13

Ross spun the car into the hospital car park, pulling up in front of the entrance and allowing Macleod to jump out. He ran towards A&E, bursting in to see a small number of people waiting calmly. He went over to the window where a formidable-looking nurse sat looking at him.

'You just brought in a Councillor Morgan; I need to know how he is.'

'Okay, and who are you, sir?'

Macleod reached inside his coat, pulled out his credentials, and held them up at the window, 'Detective Inspector Seoras Macleod. I need to know how the councillor is.'

'If you'll sit and wait, I'll just go and find out for you, sir.'

'Can you let me in so I can go and see?'

'No,' said the woman, 'I'm afraid not. If Councillor Morgan is being worked on, we need to give them space. I hope you understand that.'

'But I need to know what happened with the man. It may be my only chance to talk to him.'

'I appreciate what you're saying, sir, but it's quite strict at the moment. You won't get in if he's in there being worked on.'

There was a tap on Macleod's shoulder, and he turned

around with a disgruntled face to see Jona Nakamura. 'Seoras,' she said, 'leave it to me. Okay? Go and sit down and I'll get you through if he's capable of speaking.'

Jona stepped in front of Macleod and smiled at the woman. Macleod went over to where everyone was sitting down, forced himself to sit, and tried to ignore the children's television programs that were on the TV just above his head. As Ross came into the accident and emergency section, having parked the car, Macleod was astonished as Jona was led through into the A&E. Macleod saw the door click behind her and he sat twiddling his thumbs.

'What's happening, sir?' asked Ross.

Macleod stood up and took Ross to one side, whispering to him, 'They're not letting me through; it appears they're working on Councillor Morgan. I don't know how, but Jona's got herself in. She said she'd call us if the guy was capable of speaking.'

'So, I guess it's sit-and-wait time then.'

'No. It's time to get hold of the others.' Macleod picked up his phone calling Hope.

'Hey, Seoras, it's Hope.'

'Councillor Morgan's collapsed. They've got him here by ambulance. I'm standing in A&E at the moment. Jona's through with him, but it looks like he's not speaking. Start getting a team together. I want a search done of our suspects' houses. Locate them all, then check Annie Spencer's house, Sarah MacIver's, and Innes Stewart's . . .and also Joy Grundy's. Check their persons as well.'

'You're looking for thallium poison?'

'Well, that's all I've got to go on now. Jona hasn't come back, but I don't want to wait. You might be able to intercept some of them before they reach their houses. Clarissa is still out there. Get on the phone to her pronto, and Sergeant Dolan as well. I'm going to stay here and see what Jona says.'

Macleod returned to sit down on a seat and looked over at a smiling child. The child looked up, pointed to the screen, and then began to dance in a mimic of what a furry character on screen was doing. The child's mother looked closely at Macleod, but Macleod didn't flinch, thinking through in his mind what was going on. He could hear the whispered words of 'miserable bugger', but he didn't care.

*What is going on here?* he thought. This was potentially a third body. Up until now, he had in his mind that there could be an affair between Donald MacDonald and Miranda Folly, and Joy Grundy was certainly presenting as a possible suspect. Councillor Morgan too was an option, although Macleod wasn't sure the man had it in him, but he was now heading into hospital. Somebody had taken care of Morgan. Maybe it was to do with what light he could shed. He said he hadn't spoken to anyone in the family about revealing the possible affair that was going on, but he didn't say if he'd spoken to someone else about it. Maybe somebody else knew and was covering tracks.

Macleod waited for over an hour and had sent Ross back in the meantime to the station to help coordinate the searches. It was as he was despairing of ever getting through to A&E that Jona Nakamura appeared at the door, was buzzed out, and strode over to Macleod.

'Don't kick up a fuss, Seoras,' she said quietly. 'You can come in, but I'm afraid he never regained any consciousness.'

Macleod nodded and was led through by Jona into a private cubicle where he saw Councillor Morgan lying on a table. His clothes had been cut away and his face looked at peace with the eyes closed.

'What killed him?' asked Macleod.

'Well, it's a little early to say,' said Jona, 'but my guess is thallium and a lot of it. This looks like a significant dose.'

'He was just in the coffee shop. They all were. They'd all come back. I was sat talking to him not that long beforehand. I didn't see anybody put anything in his coffee, but then again . . .'

'What?' asked Jona.

'Well, I got up to the bathroom. I must have been in there ten minutes.'

'Ten minutes?'

'Yes, I was thinking,' said Macleod.' I was in the cafe with Morgan and Grundy and I had to get out and think, so I stayed in the toilet for ten minutes. Then, I came back out, and the man was gone.'

'What happened during that time though?' asked Jona.

'I don't know. Get on with what you're doing,' said Macleod, 'and I'll phone the others. They were there, too.'

Macleod exited A&E and stood outside with his phone.

'Hope,' he said when his sergeant had picked up the phone, 'in the coffee house, I was talking to Morgan. You were talking to Sarah MacIver. I got up and went to the toilet. What happened during that period of time?'

'Don't know,' said Hope. 'I was interviewing Sarah. My back was to Morgan. I don't know if anybody went near him or not.'

'We need to find out. Get Dolan down to start interviewing customers that were there. Interview the couple as well. Get a search done in the coffee house. See if we can find out if there's any traces of thallium. Jona will be down shortly, but I reckon we can get her deputy down.'

'Will do. Have you tried Clarissa?'

'She's my next call. Where is she?'

'She's out searching the houses. I think she got into Annie Stewart's, which is more than what I did, but there are others working their way round. They haven't come up with anything, Seoras. They haven't found anything.'

'Okay,' said Macleod, 'just keep going on it. Something's going to break soon.'

He placed a call to Clarissa Urquhart but the response was very similar. Clarissa had been engaged with a suspect and had been talking to Innes Stewart, not particularly paying any attention to Morgan seeing that Macleod was with him. In fact, she was struggling to remember exactly when Morgan had left. When he called Hope back, she said it was just before Macleod had come back out of the bathroom.

He stood outside the hospital looking, thinking to himself. *There was a chance.* He put repeat calls into Clarissa and Hope asking if their suspects moved during those ten minutes he was in the bathroom. Both remembered them getting up and approaching the serving area but then they turned back checking phones, looking to see if anybody was contacting them. They couldn't say for definite that neither suspect had gone anywhere near Councillor Morgan.

It was an hour later when Macleod got back down to the police station, choosing to walk it, trying to see if any ideas would come to him. When he rolled into the operations room, Ross waved him over.

'Sir, we've looked at everything; I've had teams go through all the houses—we've got nothing. There's a couple of colourless

115

liquids that we took, but they've been tested and they're not thallium. So far, we have nothing. We've tried to see who was on the move and to be honest, everybody got up in those ten minutes. It appeared Councillor Morgan knew most of them. We tried to recover his coffee cup, but it's been washed.'

'It may not have been done at the club,' said Macleod. 'We should trace his movements beforehand.'

'Have done, was with his wife all morning. Hadn't been anywhere else.'

*She's got no reason to see off, has she?* thought Macleod. *She's not even in the picture when it comes to the other two.* Macleod marched over to his desk, sat down, and put his feet up on it, and sat looking at the far wall.

'What do we do now, sir?' asked Ross.

'Go over it again, Ross. Pull out the files, see who saw anyone. Give me times when people were there. Did the statements collaborate them? See if we can take anyone out of our picture. I need to narrow this down.'

'We can't say for definite that the poison was administered in the club.'

'No, we can't. We can't say anything for definite. I'm looking for coincidences, and then we need to nail it down. We need to work out who did this.'

'Of course, sir,' said Ross and shifted out of the inspector's reach, realising that Macleod was becoming agitated. As he sat at his desk, Macleod's phone rang and he picked it up.

'Inspector, it's Joy Grundy. I've just heard about Councillor Morgan.'

'If you're not going to give me information or confess to his murder,' said Macleod, 'then really, this call is inappropriate.'

Joe Grundy seemed to ignore him, 'You must be feeling

dreadful that sort of thing happening. You were probably there. Heck, I was there.'

'I'm well aware you were there, Miss Grundy. You're a suspect, so kindly, unless you've got information to give me, get off the phone.'

'Inspector, you must be feeling dreadful. If you get time this evening, feel free to pop around. We can open a bottle of wine. I'm a very good listener. Maybe you need a bit of relaxation. After all, Jane's quite far away.'

Macleod grabbed the phone tighter to his ear, 'Look, Miss Grundy, the last thing I need is a dinner date with you.'

The eyes of the station flew over to Macleod, but no one said a word.

'Unless you have information to give me or are admitting to any of these murders, kindly put the phone down.'

'Inspector, I'm quite good at relaxation techniques.'

Macleod slammed the phone down so hard that a constable across from him jumped. 'Back to work,' he said. 'Let's find them—find who's doing this.'

Ross stood up and looked at the others around him, 'You heard the inspector. Nose to the grindstone; come on, people.'

Macleod realised that Ross had put it better and diffused a moment when their leader was seemingly out of control. Macleod stood up and marched across to the filter coffee machine, pouring himself one, and then he turned round to everyone else. 'Does anybody else want one?'

There was a voice behind him, 'It's very generous but it is so unlike you it's ridiculous. You don't need to apologise to them for being riled.'

Hope was correct but Macleod shrugged his shoulders, took his drink, and marched back to his desk. Hope made her way over, stood in front of it, put two hands on the desk, and looked at Macleod.

'I think this might be a bad time to tell you,' said Hope, 'but A, we found nothing, B, we can't make anything link, and C, we've got the press downstairs looking for a statement.'

'The press? We don't need the press.'

'You need to take this one, Seoras,' said Hope quietly. 'They're going to run a piece about you being bested.'

'What? What do you mean, being bested?'

'Saying this is a perfect murder. You don't know how it happened or what's going on. Got a statement from someone in A&E saying you were agitated, didn't even entertain her child when he smiled at you.'

'I'm running a murder enquiry,' said Macleod, 'not a nursery.'

'That might be true,' said Hope, 'but they'll spin it their way.'

'They'll spin it their way, whatever.'

'Trust me on this one, Seoras. You need to go down. Just tell them enquiries are ongoing. Can't say too much lest something gets out of the bag, that sort of thing. Keep your cool. Do that face you do when you've got it solved.'

'The face I do when I've got it solved?' queried Macleod.

'Yes,' said Hope, 'the slightly smug one. The one that sits and plays cards all night. The one that nobody can break into. That one.'

'You make me sound like a bit of a—'

'Prig?' said Hope. 'There's times you've gone off and solved things without telling me, so yes, Seoras, frankly,' and she bent forward in a whisper and said, 'you can be a right prig, but at the moment, you need to be downstairs and telling these people everything's fine.'

'Of course, you're right,' said Macleod.

'If we weren't in company, I'd rub the knot out of those shoulders,' said Hope. 'Why is Jane never around when I need her?'

'Don't,' said Macleod, 'I've just had Joy Grundy invite me for dinner.'

'Dinner?' said Hope, then realised she said it quite loud. 'Why is she inviting you for dinner?'

'She's either the worst criminal I've ever seen or she just, I don't know, has a crush on me.'

'A crush? That's what school girls get. Are you sure she isn't playing us, playing you?'

'If she's playing me, it's not working,' said Macleod, 'because it's not like I'm going for dinner.'

'So where do we go from here?' asked Hope.

'Well, I'm going downstairs to speak to some reporters and I'm putting on that face that makes it look like I know everything. You and Clarissa are back out. This will be solved amongst these people. I'm convinced that's where it's happening. It's too much of a coincidence that everybody's arriving same place every day. Go find out what's going on.'

Macleod watched Hope walk away and then stood up, adjusted his tie, and made sure his coat was on properly. He then went to make a move downstairs when Ross came up to him.

'Just to let you know, sir, we've gone through with no sign of thallium anywhere. The cafe is clean. Their houses are clean. They're clean.'

'Well, thank you, Ross,' said Macleod, 'I'll just pop downstairs and tell the press that we're bamboozled, no idea what's going on.'

'Well, it's either that or make something up, sir,' said Ross.

119

Macleod raised an eyebrow and left for his press conference.

# Chapter 14

Hope departed the police station, walking along the Stornoway streets until she came to the house of Sarah MacIver. It was a small flat sitting atop another flat in what was considered a cheaper part of town. Most people in the house were renting from the council. Sarah's house looked like no exception.

As Hope made it to the front door, she opened it to find stairs up to two flats at the top. There were two doors at the bottom for the lower flats. Sarah's was the top-right. Hope climbed the rather bland staircase up to a wooden door that simply said, 'D.' Rapping the door because there was no sign of a doorbell, Hope heard a shout of 'In a minute' from inside. The door opened, and Sarah MacIver stood drying her hair with a dressing gown on.

'Oh,' she said, 'it's you again. I was just having a shower, going to settle down for the night. Not much happening.'

'Do you mind if I come in and ask a few more questions?'

'Not at all,' said Sarah, 'please do,' and she stepped to one side, an arm held out allowing Hope to enter.

'What's it like being a detective inspector?'

'I wouldn't know,' said Hope turning to smile at the girl. 'I'm a detective sergeant. My boss, Macleod, he's the inspector.'

'He's quite old, isn't he?' said Sarah. 'Surely, you'll be taking over one day.'

'Maybe one day,' said Hope. 'It doesn't always work like that. Why do you ask?'

'Must be exciting. Seeing all these murders and that. Though, in some ways, it must be quite glamorous, standing in front of the press, doing all these briefings, your face on the telly.'

'I think you should sit down with my boss and ask him how glamorous it is. I think he'd put you straight.'

'Really?' said Sarah. 'I think there's something dramatic about it, isn't there?'

'It's dramatic enough that Constable Ross, who I'm in charge with, has been shot on duty. I've had my fair few kickings, and so has my boss. A few times, things have cut close.' Sarah looked up at Hope, staring distinctly at her cheek. 'That came from saving the boss's wife—acid,' said Hope.

'Pity,' said Sarah, 'you've quite a photogenic face.'

'It's not to be pitied,' said Hope. 'The boss said it's one of the most beautiful things about me.'

'Well, each to their own,' said Sarah, and Hope realised she really hadn't caught the meaning. 'If you just give me a minute,' said Sarah, 'I need to do my hair. I'll be back out then.'

Hope nodded, and started to walk around the living room, looking around her. Everywhere she stared were pictures of different men and women posing in front of large landscapes. As Hope peered at them closely, she realised that whoever took the photographs was quite good. Hope looked over to her dresser and realised that there were a few albums there.

She picked one up and started flicking through it. Again, there were more photographs, women in stylish clothes, smart dressed men in suits. Although she looked at them and saw that most had a local tinge to them, out in the moorland, in Stornoway, areas she recognised by the harbour, the War Memorial, or out by the peat bank. *Still, they were well taken*, she thought and picked up more to scan through.

There were recurring features in the men and women at the post, but there was enough variety for Hope to realise that none of them were probably anybody to Sarah. They were simply a model employed for the day. Hope pulled out the next one and looked through, again believing they all looked rather well. As she got to the bottom album, Hope recognised that they were all of a similar vein.

She pulled the drawer at the bottom of the dresser and saw another album. This one was chunky. It also had no label on it. The others had said things like, *Photographs of life form. Action shots*, but this one had no label. Hope opened it, looked inside, and saw the face of Miranda Folly.

*It was indeed a radiant shot*, Hope thought, *with the hair coming down around the woman's face, that she did really look quite something*. However, Hope was quite shocked by the lack of clothing beneath that. In fairness, the picture was tasteful, although a nude. Hope wasn't really shocked, but rather intrigued that Miranda was posing for Sarah. She continued to flick through. The more she looked, the more she realised that the photographs, although tasteful, were quite provocative. Clearly there to turn on whoever was looking at them.

'Dear God. No,' said Sarah, 'that's not what you think it is.'

'I wasn't thinking it was anything,' said Hope, turning around and finding Sarah emerging from a room in her pyjamas and dressing gown. 'You handle a camera very well.'

'I don't tend to show those ones,' said Sarah, 'not really to anyone. They were handed in for a project, a part of my course. I do some photography in it, but it's more to do with art. I also drew a lot of those photographs afterwards and other media.'

'It's very good. I am a little intrigued though,' said Hope. 'Forgive me for asking, but why is Miranda Folly the only nude model in this?' Sarah blushed. 'It's all right. You can tell me,' said Hope, 'I'm a Detective Sergeant. Unless it's relevant to the case, this will go no further. If it's relevant to the case, it'll go to my DI. Just tell me, if you have nothing to fear.'

'What do you mean nothing to fear?'

'She's dead. Someone killed her,' said Hope. 'If it wasn't you, just let me know what this is all about because you never mentioned this link. You said Miranda sat in the corner. She didn't talk to people. She clearly talked to you.'

Hope watched the girl shy away and skulk towards the kitchen area, at the far end of the flat. She opened the cupboard, took out a bottle of wine, grabbed a corkscrew, and pulled the bottle open. She took out a glass and poured a rather large measure before turning to Hope.

'I'm on duty. No,' said Hope.

'Can you just ask another question?' Sarah took her glass, gulped down about half of it before putting the glass back on the table. 'Look, it's quite simple, I had a project up at the college. I had to look at glamour modelling. I basically went about it by getting someone to do it. It was an exploration of how the photographs are different. I didn't go very far with it. You can see they're all tasteful. It wasn't that long ago you could have put them in the paper and nobody would've batted an eyelid.'

'Oh, I think they're better than that,' said Hope. 'It's just

124

quite a lot implied in them, and they're very good. You could probably make a lot of money doing that.'

'Do you think so?' said Sarah, suddenly warming.

'I do, but it's not answering my question. Why are they of Miranda Folly?'

'It's kind of awkward to get someone who's going to do that sort of thing. You don't want somebody too young. I mean my friends would just be idiots about it. Then if you get somebody too young, it looks like you're actually trying to do it properly, but they also don't pose right. Also, here, can you imagine if this ever got found out? They were very discreet at the college. My assessor took them, gave them back, didn't keep any of them. I made that a condition of giving them to her.'

'Very wise,' said Hope. 'Was Miranda okay with them going in?'

'It was a bit strange finding Miranda to do it,' said Sarah, and again, she started to redden. 'I thought about who I know, who's quiet enough, and discreet enough. I'd seen Miranda sitting in the Cortado club every day and look at her. She's a fabulous-looking woman, a bit older. She wasn't serious about herself, thought it strange I asked, but she put a lot of effort into the shoots.'

'What made you think she might go for it though?' asked Hope.

'I probably shouldn't say, but I quite like her books.'

'You've read some of them?' said Hope.

'Yes, and I saw a YouTube clip of her at a conference and was stunned that that was actually Miranda. That's the Miranda I know. One day in the Cortado Club, I went up to her, whispered in her ear about it, and she told me to sit down beside her. We talked quite briefly about it, but we got

125

overheard.'

'Oh,' said Hope, 'by who?'

'Joy bloody Grundy, and you know what, she actually asked me if she could pose. Can you believe that? She's a churchwoman and that. I actually believe if I had shot her, she would've wanted the photographs to be seen. She was really pushy. For a couple of days, she was coming in, and I mean the stuff she was wearing. It'd look trashy on an 18-year-old, but on her it just looked ridiculous. Not that Donald minded. He was eyes everywhere because Joy kept coming over to me, and then she'd go over to Miranda. She'd give her hell about stuff without actually saying what.'

'Did Miranda retaliate?'

'No, she said nothing, but she came and she worked for me and that book is what we did. The album got handed in, it was assessed, it was given back. Now, it sits in the bottom of that drawer. I'm very proud of the photos,' said Sarah. 'Really proud of them. It's just in a place like this, it's not going to float, is it?'

'I suppose not,' said Hope.

'Especially now,' said Sarah. 'Can you imagine?'

'Did anybody else know she was doing this for you, other than Joy?'

'Not as far as I'm aware. Joy thought Donald knew. I can't say that was true. If Donald was having a thing with Miranda, who knows? Miranda never asked for him to come along. All the things we did were just her and me privately. You can see most of them are her house, are just out the back garden, not beyond. We didn't get to go on location. Last thing we wanted was to be caught. The rumour mill on this island and that.'

'You say it lasted what, three weeks?'

'Three weeks because I had a deadline. At the end of it, we shook hands. She never asked for any copies, said she just enjoyed doing it. I think she may have done it as research.'

'Research?' asked Hope.

'One of her books, one of the characters, turns to posing for someone and does the same sort of thing. I think that's why she did it. The start of that book, it says, 'A special thank you to Sarah.' Doesn't give my full name, but that's for me. She never told me. Not sure she knew I read her books, but maybe that's what she suspected when I came to her.'

'This is important, Sarah. I'm going to ask it again,' said Hope. 'Did anybody else know? Is there any possibility anybody else could have overheard?'

'No, I don't think so.'

'What about Counsellor Morgan?' said Hope.

'No, not from me. Don't think from Miranda either. Unless Donald told him about Miranda maybe, but Donald never saw the photographs.'

'Did you always have the photographs? Did you have them at all times before you handed them in? How much do you trust the assessor you give them to?'

'I trust her implicitly. She was quite determined that they shouldn't go anywhere.'

'What's her name?'

'Miss Cohen. She's not from here. She's from off-island, but she's been here quite a time. I think she would understand what it would mean for it to get out.'

'I'm going to check that up just to make sure that the book didn't go anywhere else. Other than that, you never had the book out of your sight?'

'Give me a moment,' said Sarah and took the glass of wine

again, this time finishing the rest of it. 'God, did I? Do you really think this is involved?'

'I don't know what's involved. All I know is we've got three people. I'm seeking anything that ties them together.'

'Two nights, I didn't have it,' said Sarah. 'There were two nights I didn't have it. I gave her the finished folder. It was after it had been assessed and that, and it came back to me before I put it in the drawer. I was in the coffee house and remember this is a while back now. We're talking nearly a year. She asked me for it, and I gave it to Miranda. Just two nights, said she wanted to look at it again. Said she was feeling rather low, needed a boost.'

'Did she seem rather low?' asked Hope.

'No. In some ways, the next two days, I thought she was rather excited.'

'Is there any possibility she could have shared it with Donald?'

'Who knows,' said Sarah. 'He's a married man. If the two of them were playing away, so to speak, he's not going to share stuff like that.'

'Could he have shared it with Counsellor Morgan?'

'I don't know,' said Sarah, suddenly turning away. 'I don't know. Hang on a minute. Do you think I'm at risk?'

'I don't know,' said Hope. 'I'm trying to string together possible connections and so far, this is a pretty strong one. It's pretty conclusive that Donald MacDonald and Miranda Folly were having an affair. Donald's best friend is Counsellor Morgan. Some people say he didn't see it, but some people say he was jealous. We don't know.'

'Should I be careful?'

'Careful?' said Hope. 'You drink at an establishment where

three people have died and you're usually there when they're there. Yeah, I'd be careful.'

'I'm not having my life dictated to though,' said Sarah. 'I won't go for that.'

Hope rolled her eyes. *That is the trouble of people nowadays. Won't have their life dictated to. Somebody was poisoning people, killing them right there and so far, three people haven't stopped it. Nobody had noticed it happening and yet this young woman, she wasn't going to have her life dictated to. Who is dictating? Just keep your head low for two weeks until the police sort it out. Unbelievable*, thought Hope, *All she's got to do is stay up at the college during her break.*

'I think you should stay up at the college during your break.'

'No,' said Sarah. 'They won't dictate to me. It's my life. It's what I do. I'm not having it.'

'You go against my advice, you run the risk of possibly getting pulled into this. I've warned you to the best that I know. I don't know the connections; I don't know why people are dying at the moment. I've warned you, so, on your own head, be it,' said Hope. With that, she turned to walk out the door when she stopped and looked back. 'They're very good pictures though,' said Hope. 'If I was ever to do something like that, I'd hope I'd get a photographer like you.' She shut the door behind her.

# Chapter 15

Clarissa sat in the Cortado Club, having reorganised its opening, making sure that Jona had finished examining the scene. The forensic lead had worked all night and the club was late opening before she managed to pull out the last of her team. Macleod had sent Clarissa down to deal with Boris in case he wasn't happy at not being allowed to open first thing in the morning. The man was up in arms saying that he needed to get the club open, but Clarissa stood firm. Then, when the club opened just after ten, she decided to sit down for a coffee.

In truth, the team were perplexed. There didn't seem to be a definitive theme to what was happening. Sure, Joy Grundy was a strong suspect, but it all seemed very circumstantial. There was nothing to pin it on the woman. No one had seen her plant the thallium into any drink; no one could find any thallium around her house or on her person.

Clarissa could see the boss was getting worried. It wasn't like Macleod. When she left the station that morning, there were more TV crews waiting outside looking for a statement. In truth, over recent years, Macleod had been on the television more than he'd like and he'd been turning into some sort of a celebrity. Not well known and certainly not invited onto any TV game shows, but Clarissa reckoned that a good proportion of the population would know his face when it appeared on the screen.

In her own mind, it didn't seem to follow that Joy Grundy would actually poison people. There was no fit of rage to her. The woman was so bubbly, lively, and when Macleod described how she approached him, she never seemed to take offense. So what if Donald had decided on Miranda instead? Clarissa's opinion was that Joy would keep trying on the off chance, but she didn't look like a one-man woman. Joy was more about herself, about being loved, rather than loving. It just didn't fit for Clarissa. The desperation of wanting to pose for photographs, in some ways, made Clarissa pity her. She certainly wouldn't be caught doing that.

When Clarissa next looked at her watch, it was heading towards eleven, and she realised that Innes Stewart had just entered. She smiled over at the man, and he gave her a courteous nod before making his way up to buy his coffee. Shortly after, Clarissa saw the student, Sarah MacIver, enter, set up at a table, and flip her laptop up. As she was in, Clarissa thought best that she stay there, keep an eye out on what was going on. Maybe she would get a chance to work out what was happening. It was then that Annie Spence walked in and made a beeline over to Clarissa.

'That sergeant of yours called round.'

'Sergeant?' asked Clarissa, 'You mean, Detective Sergeant Hope McGrath?'

'Yes. What rank are you?'

The woman looked a little bit strange, and her eyes pierced into Clarissa. Clarissa took a defensive posture.

131

'I'm actually a Detective Sergeant as well. Did you want to speak to Sergeant McGrath?'

'I told her I wanted Macleod. Macleod's the one I want. He's the one on the telly, isn't he? Macleod, he's here.'

'Detective Inspector Macleod is running the operation, yes.'

'Let's have Macleod then,' said Annie. 'Go and tell Macleod.'

'I'll let Inspector Macleod know that you're looking for him, but you can tell me if you want.'

The woman waved her hands. 'No, Macleod.'

'Is it something pressing you need to tell him?'

'Macleod. I want to speak to Macleod.'

Clarissa sighed; the woman must be half daft. 'Okay,' said Clarissa, 'when I go back, I'll inform Inspector Macleod to come to your house. Will that do you?'

'Macleod though. I don't want that woman again. She's not of the same standing, like you, she's a minor detective.'

Clarissa could feel her shoulders rise, but then she let it go and almost laughed in the woman's face. 'I'll let the great Macleod know you're looking for him. Now, if you don't mind, I'm quite busy.'

Clarissa bent down and drank some more of her coffee. She decided to stay and watch as Annie made her way back to the table. She realised one thing, though, she'd lost track of the other two suspects. Although she realised that Joy Grundy had walked in as well, so the four of them were now here, and Clarissa thought it best to stay, keep an eye out, see how they behaved. That's what Macleod had said: they'd find it in the person, not in the records.

Clarissa never quite understood how he came to these ideas. She was someone who charged after things, hunted them down, pushed, shook, and rattled people till the truth came out.

Macleod got beyond that. He was seeing the answer before they even spoke.

She knew it annoyed Hope. The sergeant was not on the same level. Clarissa reckoned you couldn't teach that thing; it was just an inherent ability the man had in the same way as you couldn't teach him to chill out more. *He's a right stuck-up pompous ass at times*, she thought. Then, she smiled.

It had been good since she joined the team. Certainly, a change from the art world, and she'd seen some things she'd rather not. Then again, on a murder team, she guessed that was par for the course.

She drank the last of her coffee, looked around again at her suspects, and thought about ordering another one because they hadn't left. As she waved over Boris, she noticed Annie was stumbling. The woman had stood up in a very unbalanced fashion and was now making her way across the entire cafe and directly towards Clarissa.

'Macleod,' shouted the woman. 'Macleod. You need Macleod,' she was holding her stomach, and then her head, and then she was moving this way and that.

Suddenly, the woman toppled forward, and Boris dropped Clarissa's coffee, reaching out for Annie as she fell. He caught her, but the woman's eyes were closed, and Clarissa instructed him to put her down on her back. She bent down checking for a pulse and there was one. The woman was murmuring, making no sense.

'Boris, 999, ambulance now.'

The owner nodded his head and shouted over to his wife, and Clarissa tried to cradle Annie's head. She then put her into the recovery position, worried in case the woman would be sick, would possibly choke on her vomit. Clarissa felt her stomach tighten. She really didn't know what was happening.

Clarissa had never seen someone poisoned and she was unsure quite how it would take effect. There are so many different poisons in the world, but what she did know was that she should keep talking to the woman.

'You want Inspector Macleod, is that right? Annie, talk to me. Who is it you want?'

'Macleod. I need Macleod, Macleod will solve it. Macleod's the genius. You can't beat Macleod. They said you'll never beat Macleod.'

Clarissa continued to talk to Annie asking her where she lived, but slowly the woman began to fade away and she became less responsive. The ambulance crew were quick. Once inside, they started to take care of Annie and she was soon whisked out of the shop, at which point, Clarissa grabbed her phone and rang Macleod.

'I'm just about to go to a press conference,' said Macleod. 'Can't have another one. Get to the hospital. I'll be with you soon as.'

Clarissa ran as quick as she could back to the station. Because the café was only a short distance away, she hadn't bothered bringing her car down. When she made it to the hospital, she found Macleod had beaten her.

'I thought you had the press conference.'

'Hope's doing it. I thought it was more important to be here. What happened?'

Clarissa began to talk through her morning and told of how Annie collapsed as the two of them stood in A&E off to one corner. It wasn't a busy time with only one other person waiting but Macleod still kept a distance because he didn't want any details becoming public knowledge.

'Did you shut the place down?'

'I told Boris to lock up before I left,' said Clarissa. Macleod picked up his phone and rang Ross.

'Get yourself down there, Ross, lock it up so Jona's people can get there. I want to see if there's any thallium around. It looks like she's been poisoned.'

'Are you sure?' asked Ross. 'She hasn't just collapsed? She is quite old from my records.'

'Just get down and close the place up, Ross.'

*That was techy*, thought Clarissa. 'Are you okay, Seoras?' she asked quietly.

'Splendid,' said Macleod.

'Enough of that,' said Clarissa. 'Don't play the moody arse with me. What's up?'

'We haven't got anything, but every time I go out there, I get asked what have we got, what have we got, and we've got nothing, except some woman who likes to think of herself as the centre of attention. It's not strong enough, Clarissa, not strong enough. There's no evidence to back it up. It's all circumstantial. Every time I go up there, I have to just say we're looking for more leads, asking for the public to come forward. How much of the public do we need? They were all sat in the ruddy coffee house.'

The last words had begun to get louder, and Clarissa put her hand on Macleod's shoulder, 'Easy, not the place. If you want to vent, go somewhere else. Look, I get it, it can't be easy with all the publicity you got recently. Especially the rescue on the boat.' She gripped Macleod, 'They never really said much about Hope, did they? I thought they would.'

'What do you mean?' asked Macleod.

'Well, Hope, look at her. She's made to be on the front cover

135

of a magazine. She should be on there on the telly. Looks better than you.'

'She's not the boss. They don't say her name when they talk about a case. They say DI Macleod's on it. That's what they say, Clarissa. They don't say Urquhart's there. I run this as a team. Sometimes you come through with stuff, sometimes it's Hope. Ross picks up a load of spadework and gets no credit for it outside of the team. It's all about Macleod and Macleod's team. Hence when it doesn't go well, it comes on me.'

'Jona's trying to get your attention,' said Clarissa looking through the glass doors that led further into the A&E. Macleod went over followed by Clarissa, and Jona let them in, taking them through to a side room where they could see Annie resting.

'How is she?'

'She's going to be okay,' said Jona. 'It was thallium poisoning. We determined it reasonably quickly, got an antidote into her, but there's something I'm not following here.'

'What?' asked Macleod.

'The last one, Councillor Morgan, the dose was so big, we wouldn't have had a chance. I suspect with Donald MacDonald, it was the same. Who knows with Miranda? There wasn't much with Annie. They must have missed. They must have not got enough into the coffee or however they were passing it on.'

'Is she going to be okay here? Are you needed any longer?'

'Not up here, Seoras,' said Jona.

'Right, Ross has locked down that coffee house. I want you down there. I want every inch of that place gone over again.'

'Of course,' said Jona, 'on my way.'

'Find me something,' said Macleod, 'find me what it is.' His voice was almost angry, and Clarissa stood back in shock. 'Inspector,' said Jona, 'can I have you for a minute alone?'

'Of course,' said Macleod, waving off Clarissa. She stepped out of the room but made sure she was still within earshot.

'Seoras, don't ever speak to me like that again. I don't know what's up with you, but you don't tell me to find something with forensics. Every time I go, I do the job thoroughly. What's there to be found will get found. If it's not there, it won't. Never, ever insist on things like that.'

'Sorry,' said Macleod. 'I'm just on edge. It's not your fault. You didn't deserve that. Of course, you'll find what's there. If you'd go down and just have a hunt for me.'

'Of course,' said Jona. 'It's not all on you. You realise that, don't you?'

'Feels like it.'

Clarissa watched Macleod wait for a moment while Jona passed her giving a smile. When the inspector came out, Clarissa joined him, and he spoke to the doctor who advised it would be a while before Annie would be available to talk to. Macleod said he would be back, and in the meantime, suggested that they should return to the station to have a conference about what was going on. They needed some new angle, some new way of looking at things.

When they returned to the station, Macleod called a meeting in half an hour, asking his three other detectives to join him in a side room. While she was waiting, Clarissa answered a phone call from Jona.

'You better tell Macleod,' said Jona, 'I found the thallium. It was beside her cup. It looks like somebody missed. The woman was darn lucky. I would suggest there was enough in the dose that didn't go into the cup to kill her. She hadn't finished her coffee fully, and she clearly took a strong reaction to it. I'm a little bit surprised at the speed, but given her previous medical history, which I saw from the doctor, it's entirely possible she reacted strongly with the thallium.'

Clarissa took the news to Macleod, entering the room where her three colleagues were waiting for her.

'You're late,' said Macleod.

'Two minutes, Seoras. Give us a break,' said Clarissa, 'and besides, I was talking to Jona. She says thallium's present on the saucer beside the cup that Annie was drinking out of, said it looks like they missed with the big dose. Said her reaction to it was quick, but given her medical history, that wasn't unreasonable.'

Macleod stood up and strode to the window. 'Okay,' he said, 'let's hear what else you got.'

# Chapter 16

W ell, sir,' said Ross, 'after going into the background records, I'm struggling.'

'Struggling?' said Macleod. 'It's not what I want to hear. Struggling to find records or struggling to find something incriminating?'

'Something incriminating, sir. The trouble is every one record I go into, they don't seem to have done anything illegal in their life. Sarah MacIver's just started out. As far as I can see, her bank balance is fine. She's just a student, not got a lot of money. Miranda Folly, other than she writes quite erotic books, again, perfect record. She's not done anything deviant in her life. Donald MacDonald, family man, seems fine as well. No issues in the background. Counsellor Morgan, you go into the council stories, there's nothing jumping out at me. He's voted several times, a bit on controversial issues, but none of them seemed to have come back. There are no real big stories about them. He seems to be one of those affable counsellors getting on here because of his church connections quite often.'

'Church connections?' said Macleod.

'Yes. When you look at his canvasing brochure from last time, or rather his statement to get into the council, half of it was taken up with the church connections. I'd imagine that could go down quite well here.'

'Sad to say it, Ross, but yes, quite often your connections stand for a lot here.'

'It's not only like that on the island though, is it, Seoras?' said Hope.

Macleod didn't seem to be appeased. 'No, it's not. Just here, Hope,' said Macleod, 'the difference is quite stark, this is the place that tells everyone else how to run things, how perfect the island is, how perfect our churches are. I grew up in that hypocrisy, remember?'

'I think you might be overstating it, Seoras.'

'Overstating it? My wife died because of it.'

There was a silence in the room and Macleod turned away to the window. A few moments later, he turned back. 'Sorry. You're right in what you're saying. I'm just a little on edge.'

'A lot on edge,' said Clarissa. 'It's us four. Ease down. You nearly tore Jona apart for nothing.'

Macleod thumped the table. 'What is it? What's going on here? What about the owners, Ross?'

'Well, there is an issue there. Boris is in trouble to a point. The café has gone well from what I can see. He's kept up on all his payments of that, but his personal account keeps having large amounts of money taken out.'

'Is he being extorted?' said Macleod.

'No, he's gambling. I mean, it's all quite clear. It's done with legit companies, and he's had several notes from them about the gambling, telling him to stop, to calm down, but that on top of opening up a new business and the money he's taken to cover that, they do need to have a good run in the next couple of years. Looking at the business, there's no reason why they

140

shouldn't, but obviously, it's a worry on his mind.'

'He did keep on going on about it this morning. Need to have it open, need to have the business open.'

'We're in the middle of winter,' said Ross. 'This isn't the time when he'd be making money anyway. I think he's just a little bit overwrought, sir, a touch like yourself.'

Macleod closed his eyes for a moment, and Ross could see him breathing deeply. Maybe the overwrought word was too much.

'Our owners don't seem to benefit from anybody dying, do they?'

'No,' said Ross. 'No, and if anything, it's harming their business. Why would you do this? Why would you kick off into something like this? It doesn't make any sense for the owners to do this. I can't see any connection for Alison Smith either. She and Boris, they seem to have a good thing going.'

'There's the obvious thing,' said Clarissa. 'Joy Grundy obviously liked Donald MacDonald, obviously liked to be seen, to be someone's favourite.'

'If that blessed woman needs interviewed again. I'm going to send somebody else.'

'No,' said Hope.

'Excuse me?' thundered Macleod.

'I said no, Seoras. I don't think she'd open up to anybody else, and I think you could play her. I think she'd tell you a lot of stuff that we wouldn't get out of her. She likes you, or rather, she seems very fond of you.'

'No, not in that way,' said Clarissa. 'She's fond of herself and she wants Seoras to like her. She wants him to adore her. That's the way she was with Donald MacDonald. That's why Miranda bothered her. She wants to be the centre of the attention. I mean, she's a church-going woman. She was going to take the risk of posing for photographs that if they were found out . . . well, how's the church going to see that one? I don't care how liberal it is.'

'But you just brought her up,' said Macleod.

'I did because we haven't got anything, and I'm traipsing over old ground and I want to make sure I'm right,' said Clarissa. 'I don't think she did it. I think she looks like someone who would do a lot to get what she wants, but she wants to be adored. If she got lifted for poisoning people, all she's going to get is the other sort of attention, loathing. I don't think she could handle that. I don't think she would have a go at Donald for liking someone else; she'd be up to compete.'

'You're both right,' said Macleod. 'I would get more out of her, Hope. Clarissa, that's what I see too. She talked to me about Jane, and I said to her extremely little, and yet she kept pushing, kept trying to put herself in that place. She actually touched my knee with hers when I was sitting, interviewing her.'

'What about Sarah MacIver then?' asked Hope. 'Could it be something to do with the photographs?'

'In what way?' asked Macleod. 'You said that was for a project, perfectly illegitimate reason.'

'Could there be others though? I mean, did she want to pose like that herself? Did she? Were there other photographs that got out of hand? Did she threaten to come out with them, say to Miranda that she would start showing them to people?'

'How did you feel when you were there?' asked Macleod.

'She just looks like a normal kid. In some ways, she was almost embarrassed by those photographs. As part of a course, it's what she had to do but she did it very thoroughly. I don't

142

think she's a very open person in a lot of ways—she's quite private. When she comes down from the college to the coffee shop, she's coming away from her course. I mean, she could sit up at the college; it wouldn't be a problem.'

'Exactly,' said Macleod. 'Was she blackmailing? How? In what way?'

'The one I certainly don't get is Innes Stewart,' said Ross. 'There's nothing there. The gun club he's with seems well run. There's been the odd bit of fracas with the council. Couple of applications and things, but nothing out of hand, nothing that seems untoward, and nothing directly about Innes Stewart. Everything I look up on him is good news. He's financially stable. He's a medallist at the Island Games. He seems well-thought-of. I spoke to his boss. He can't speak highly enough of him even though the guy is organising his own time.'

'That's the only bit I find funny,' said Clarissa, 'the way he runs his job doing everything in unsocial hours.'

'That's all around his love for someone that he thinks his family wouldn't approve of,' said Hope. 'That's what you said, wasn't it?'

'I know,' said Clarissa. 'He gave me the story that he's there. I've checked up on it, it checks out. She spoke to me. Trying to look beyond that to see if it's a cover for something else. This is the problem, isn't it, Seoras? Everybody's checking out. Everybody's good.'

'What about Annie?' asked Ross. 'I mean, she's a little old lady as far as I can see. Gets her pension, seems to enjoy coffee. Half deaf from what I gather.'

'Half deaf, ignorant. All she wants to do is talk to Macleod. Macleod this, Macleod that,' muttered Hope

'She said exactly the same to me: "Macleod, Macleod",' said

Clarissa.

'She is lying up in a hospital,' said Macleod. 'Yes, I think she will be getting to talk to Macleod, but I just don't see it. There's no angle. The only angle that makes sense at the moment is Joy Grundy, and everything about her tells me no.'

'Agreed,' said Hope, 'but we're going to have to follow it through anyway if she's the only path there.'

A police constable knocked and then opened the door, advising Macleod that there was a phone call for him. He reluctantly made his way out of the room. When he was gone, Clarissa turned to Hope. 'You've known him the longest. Is he all right?'

'The last case over in Inverness, with the big rescue on the boat, it put his face up in lights in a way it's not done before. Previously, the press were always there. Yes, his name was known, but that was massive, absolutely massive,' said Hope. 'He actually had people calling up to be on TV shows. He always plays the police guard. No, he's an inspector. That's not what he does.'

'If he ever retires though, it could work for him,' said Clarissa. 'He could be like that guy in the morning that comes on the *Breakfast Television,* the one where they try and cover a serious story with those two reporters sitting on the sofa, so they bring in somebody that actually knows what they're talking about.'

'I don't think you'll get Macleod sitting there, nice tie on, talking politely about cases somebody else is running.'

'You're right,' said Clarissa. 'He wouldn't do it because he'd probably blurt out about how they'd be getting it wrong.'

Ross laughed, and then the door opened with Macleod walking in. 'What?' he said suddenly.

'Nothing,' said Clarissa. 'We're just discussing your future

144

retirement options.'

Macleod shot her a glance. 'I'll be retired if we don't get to the bottom of this. That's the press looking for another briefing.'

'What did you do?'

'I told them you'd be down in ten minutes, and you can tell them the same thing as before. If they ask about Annie, you can tell them that she's okay, that she was taken into hospital because of complications. Tell them it's being investigated, the reason for her illness. Or maybe you could stick Clarissa's face up there as the hero dealing with her. Get mine out of the limelight.'

'You're not putting my face anywhere,' said Clarissa, 'although it would look better than yours.'

Macleod didn't seem in the mood and Hope stood up, turning to her other detectives. 'The two of you get back to it then. Tell them I'll be down to speak to them shortly, Clarissa.'

Clarissa nodded and Ross gave Hope a smile as he left the room.

'Is this your pep talk?' said Macleod.

'Seoras, you're like a prickly thornbush. Anybody says anything at the moment, you're off on one. It's not good for the team.'

'I know,' said Macleod. Hope saw him fidgeting and approach the window, looking down to the street below.

'The vans are going to be there. We go out the back as ever. This is not unusual for you. We're used to having the press about. I know you hate them, but this is enough, Seoras. Get your head in the game.'

'That's it,' said Macleod. 'Maybe this is a game.'

'What do you mean?' asked Hope.

Macleod turned away, strode back to the table and sat down looking at an empty coffee cup. 'A game, Hope, that's what it feels like. Whenever you get these murder mystery boxes, Jane says she doesn't like them because you get all these clues and it's ridiculous because anyone could've done it. It's only when you get to the conclusion and you go, 'Oh, yes. Everyone's set up.' This is like the reverse, nobody could have done it, nobody. Motive, there's only one person with a real motive. Clarissa agrees with me, and you do too when you look at it. She couldn't do it. Her nature's wrong. The style and way she goes about things, it's all wrong, it's all wrong,' said Seoras, and his hand thumped on the table again. 'This is a game, this is a game.'

'You've no evidence for that,' said Hope. 'Are you okay? There's nothing wrong with taking some time out. There's nothing wrong.'

'Don't,' said Macleod. 'Just don't. I'll be fine. Go and deal with the press. I'm just going to take a little time for myself. You're right; I've been touchy, because I've been being played. I need to get sorted. I need to get the head back on the game because that lot down in the street, they won't say anything. It's like people in the villages when the hunters came back. You can tell them all you want but until they see the carcass, they don't believe a word you say. I need to get to the bottom of this, but to do that I need to be focused.'

'Do you need my help? Do you want me to talk it through with you? Do you want to offload to me?'

'No, Hope. I want you to go and be my sergeant. I want you to take the extraneous stuff off me for the next hour. I know who I need to talk to.'

'Jona is down at the café.'

146

'Jona is quite something,' said Macleod, 'and certain things I will talk to her, but this is about me. This is about how things have been cutting against me, how this fame is reacting against me. I need to talk to someone that really understands me. Now, go, sort those reporters out.'

Hope nodded and made her way out of the room, closing the door. But as she went to go down the corridor, she stopped, turned around, and looked into the window that showed the room. Macleod had pulled his phone out and then he had it up to his ear. Hope knew who he was speaking to. Jane would be there. Jane, his partner, would sort him out.

# Chapter 17

Macleod was relishing the peace and quiet of the Western Isles Hospital as he sat waiting for the doctor to give him the go-ahead to speak to Annie Spence. The woman seemed to be doing rather well considering the fact she had collapsed, and the doctor said having been given the antidote, it was merely a matter of time of it working through her system and she should be back up on her feet very soon. In truth, the doctor said, the quantity that had been put in had caused a rather severe reaction, more than he would have expected but he said that Annie had remarkable powers of recovery and seemed to be coming back quicker than anticipated.

As Macleod sat, he felt he had renewed determination. His conversation with Jane hadn't been the most pleasant one, but she'd done what she always did, told him straight, gave him a kick up the backside, and told him to get on with it, and then she gave the promise of being there as ever when he returned. He wondered sometimes how he managed through all those years after his first wife had died until he found Jane, as he felt he couldn't be one of those men alone. It wasn't in his makeup.

It was that good old-fashioned statement, behind every good

man, there was an even better woman. He knew nowadays that that statement was quite often frowned upon because the woman was relegated out of the limelight, but in truth, he'd quite happily have Jane take the limelight at this time. He turned as the doctor emerged from Annie Spence's room.

'I think you'll be fine to speak to her, Inspector. She's doing very well. In truth, I expect her to be able to discharge tomorrow. She'll have to go home and sit and rest. Otherwise, she should be fine.'

'I think she lives on her own,' said Macleod. 'Is that really wise?'

'Are you asking that as a medical opinion or as a policeman worried about the safety of a suspect?'

'The latter, really,' said Macleod. 'Sorry, Doc. You've said your piece. If she needs protecting, then I'll organise it.'

The doctor smiled. 'You must be under a lot of pressure. It's not a problem. Hopefully, this is the last one I see in here with thallium poisoning. It's really not a forte of mine.'

'Nor of mine, Doctor, but thank you.' Macleod opened the door to Annie's room and found her sitting up on the bed, drinking a glass of water.

'Annie Spence, my name's Detective Inspector Macleod. My team say you've been asking for me.'

The woman put the cup down to one side. 'Macleod, it really is you, isn't it? My, my, Detective Inspector Macleod. You've made a name for yourself.'

'I just do my job, ma'am,' said Seoras. 'That's all any of us do. We don't look to stand in front of a film crew. That's what the press do, put us up there, trying to make more of it than what there is.'

'Oh, no. You're the hallowed Macleod. You are the man.'

The woman choked a little, grabbed her glass, and drank some more. 'I should really thank you for having one of your team there. Probably saved my life.'

'To be truthful, Annie, if I can call you Annie, you'd probably find that your life was saved by the haphazardness of the attempted killing. You see, they left a lot of the poison on the saucer of your cup.'

'Really, Inspector? So, somebody tried to kill me.'

'Somebody tried to kill you. The same person that's killed Donald MacDonald, that has killed Miranda Folly, and also Counsellor Morgan. You've been very lucky, Annie.'

'Forgive me, Inspector, I don't feel that lucky sat here. Do you know who did it?'

'That's why I'm here to speak to you, Annie. I don't understand why anyone would want to harm you. Do you have anyone that you can think of as an enemy, someone who'd be prepared to go to extremes to harm you?'

'Well, it's hard to say. I guess when you sit in that shop, you hear a lot. I'm quite quiet sitting in the corner.'

'Why do you go down every day?' asked Macleod.

'It gets me out. I see faces. I don't have much of a life. I sit in the morning watching my programs, go down, I have my coffee, come back up, have lunch, watch some more programs. I like a lot of the murder ones. Do you ever watch the detective programs?'

Macleod shook his head. 'Never. I'm a bad watch. My partner Jane watches them, but the only time I have watched one with her, I pointed out a number of glaring errors and she quickly chased me from the room,' laughed Macleod. 'But we're talking about me. That seems to be a habit of you people in that club. What about you? You say you watch the TV, so

150

you have no regular contact with anyone?'

'Just down at the Cortado Club. You see, that's why I get out.'

'Why would somebody want to kill you then? What do you know, Annie? Anything that the rest of us should know?'

Annie sat back, seeming to chew as if something was stuck in her throat. She reached over for the glass again, took a drink of water. Macleod thought she had difficulty swallowing.

'Are you okay? I could come back again if you want.'

'No,' said Annie suddenly. 'It's taken me this long to meet Macleod. The very least I can do is talk to you when you're here.'

'I do run a team. It's not that I don't want to talk to you. I can only see so many people in the day. I did send my second-in-command around, Hope McGrath, but you wouldn't speak to her.'

'She's too young to be a sergeant,' said Annie. 'I watch the programs and I like the older men, the ones who do the detecting, all very sombre, clever. Nowadays, they put these young whippersnappers in. It's just not right. They don't have that nuance, that ability to sniff the things out before they start. They say you have that. I'm not so sure, Inspector. You don't seem to have solved this one.'

Macleod began to pace at the far end of the bed. 'I ask you again, would you mind thinking if you've overheard anything that could be controversial, something that people want to cover up?'

Annie closed her eyes for a moment. Macleod for a thought that she was going off to sleep, but then suddenly, her eyes flicked open, staring at him.

'Innes Stewart,' she said, 'he comes in every day from the gun

151

club. They were talking about it. Innes said to someone that the gun club was being removed from its current site. He was quite angry about it. Very. You get to know someone when you're in there, get to know them all. You see, Macleod, Innes, all he wants is his guns. All the time about his guns. When they were talking about the gun club being moved, he was angry. Livid. In fact, he, I think he blamed the council.'

'He blamed the council. Would they have a heavy hand in it?'

'I'm an old woman, Macleod. You see that I don't get out much, so I don't know how heavy a hand. I don't read those stories. Not worth the paper they're written on. More important what you hear—that's where you get the truth of it.'

Macleod stared at the woman, weighing her up. 'Well, I'll get my sergeant to look into it.'

'You should get that older sergeant, Macleod. Get her to look at it. That young one, she couldn't even get into an old woman's house.'

'DS McGrath was being polite. She saw a frightened old woman.'

'But you don't, do you, Inspector Macleod? You see someone that knows how to listen, someone that might help you solve the case. Is that what you see, Macleod?'

Seoras was getting annoyed with the fact that the woman kept calling him Macleod. Most people would call him Inspector. If they were being formal, they might even say Inspector Macleod. His close friends called him Seoras. The only people that would call him Macleod on a routine basis were his bosses, and he kind of expected that.

Back in the day, you went by your second name, so that was taking a standard. These days, of course, the force wanted everybody on first name terms, something he found hard to adjust to, but rarely did a suspect call him Macleod. He remembered the public referred to him as Macleod.

'Is there anything else you can think of, Annie?'

'I don't think so. I hear a lot, but some of it's private.'

'Like what?'

'Well, you probably know that Joy Grundy is or was quite keen on the menfolk, especially that Donald, but he liked that Miranda. I think everyone saw that.'

'You're not telling me a lot that other people haven't said before.'

'Well,' said Annie, 'I'm going to lie down now. I need a rest. It's been quite traumatic. If you go to the council, send that other one. The older woman, not the young whippersnapper.'

'Forgive me, but I'll send who I want. I'll bid you farewell then. I may need to come back and talk to you again.'

'Whatever, Macleod.'

'Goodbye, Annie. We'll speak again.' Macleod said it in a definite way. Inside, he was sure he would need her again. On leaving the room, he picked up his phone and called Clarissa.

'Clarissa, get down to the council. There was a problem with the gun club being moved from its current site. Apparently, Innes Stewart was not keen about it. I want to find the actual reason for what was going on. Don't go down and just look at records, go and talk to the people down there. Find out from the counsellors who were at the meeting, if indeed there was one, and what civil servants were there. Get me the lowdown on it. Don't just take one person's word for it. I want a rounded opinion on what it was about.'

'Of course, Seoras, I'll get on my way.'

With the call closed, Macleod went out to the hire car and

drove it back to Stornoway Police Station. As he drove along, he remembered what Annie had said, and he'd sent Clarissa down to the council. Of course, he wouldn't send Hope. This was a minor thing, background to be checked upon. Hope was too busy coordinating everyone, making sure photos and statements were gone through, making sure the press was satisfied, and liaising with Jona.

It was how they worked. Ross took care of the absolute detail, but Hope was the one in charge of the day-to-day running. Macleod was the figurehead at the top. There it was, he thought, that again, the figurehead, the one the press hold up when really, it was a team issue. It was the team that did it.

When he returned to the office, he saw Hope and the rest of the team busy at work. When he simply gave a nod and sat down, a cup of coffee arrived for him, something he realised he took far too much for granted, but he began to chew over what he had just heard from Annie Spence.

*Macleod, always Macleod*, he thought, *like him on the telly*. He spent the next hour and a half reading through statements again, going over ground to see if anything had been missed. Hope would've done it. Ross too. Clarissa would've been through them, but it never hurt having more eyes go over them. He got up to make himself another coffee when the phone rang, and Clarissa was on the other end.

'I might have raised the riot act a little bit. They tried to throw me off, Seoras, but I pulled out the credentials. I have been in a few places and told them you were coming down if they didn't get their backside into gear.' Macleod almost laughed. 'The good news is I found out what was going on. There was a license renewal for the area where the gun club is

154

and for the usage of it as such. Apparently, this goes through as routine every so many years, but this time Joy Grundy stood up and put a complaint in about it, and Counsellor Morgan shamed her. Apparently, he was quite cutting, destroyed her in the meeting. A lot of the people I've talked to said she was quite bitter about it. It was to be one of her main things to get guns away so they couldn't be used, but Innes is a bit of a golden boy when it comes to the Island Games. Unfortunately, Joy got it in the neck, but she didn't take it well.'

'It was Counsellor Morgan, specifically, that stood up against her?'

'Very much so, I'm told. He had Innes's back, or at least the gun club's back. He has a hand in the Island Games. I think he sees it as being very worthwhile, good recognition for the island. He didn't want Innes being taken out of that. I think he was afraid that the man might disappear off to the mainland, not bother anymore.'

'So, yet another reason for Joy Grundy. More and more things seem to stack up against her. I don't like it.'

'I know what you mean, Seoras. Every time I see the woman, she doesn't look the type. We all said it the other day. She doesn't look the type.'

'No, she doesn't. Good work, Clarissa. Get yourself back here. I think we're going to have to go and talk to Joy Grundy about this.'

'Wait, sir. I think it might be wise if you go yourself, Seoras. Like we said, you might be able to get more out of her.'

'Maybe I will. Good work.'

Macleod closed down the call, sat back and thought for a moment. Joy Grundy, she'd be delighted to see him. He stood up, grabbed his coat, put it on and turned around to Hope, shouting across that he was going off to see Joy Grundy.

'Do you want me to come with you?'

'Hold the fort here. Try and dig something up. Are we missing something?'

'Not that I've seen, but clearly we are.'

Macleod nodded and made his way to the door. As he walked the corridors down to the rear entrance of the police building, all he could hear in his mind was the same word over and over again. 'Macleod, Macleod, Macleod.'

# Chapter 18

Macleod drove the car to Joy Grundy's house, heading back up the hill to the War Memorial. Having stopped at it, he heard his phone ring before he could exit the car. He picked up the call.

'Detective Inspector Macleod.'

'Inspector, it's Doctor Constance from the hospital. I just thought I'd let you know that Annie's looking to get out tomorrow morning. Said she wanted to be on her feet soon as. I reckon she's disappearing off maybe at nine in the morning. I thought you'd like to know since you were talking about protection earlier on. Might be wise for one of you to maybe pick her up.'

'That's an idea, Doctor; thank you for telling us. I'll contact my sergeant, see if she'll take her home in the morning. Expect a call.'

On closing the call, Macleod rang Hope, advising that Annie Spence would be coming out, and asked her to make her way the following morning to the hospital, but to also okay it with the doctor. Annie would be looking for hospital transport home probably, and Macleod didn't want her disappearing off on her own. Instead, if Hope went back with her, she could at least talk her through safety precautions.

Although, of course, Hope didn't even get into the house last time. This caused Macleod to smirk, but he continued his way out of the car down the path to the front door of Joy Grundy. He stood and knocked at the door and was surprised when it opened to find Joy in a Lycra top and leggings.

'Oh, excuse me, Inspector,' she said.

'I'm sorry to bother you, Miss Grundy, but I need to talk to you again. I can come back in half an hour if it's a bad time.'

Joy raised her hand to her head, wiping some sweat off her forehead. Her hair was pulled back and tied up, and she reached back untying it, and shook it out.

'Not a problem, Inspector. I'm sure you don't mind seeing me like this.'

There again, that little come on, that little push forward to see if Macleod would react.

'It's probably better if you showered and changed, and I come back in half an hour.'

'No, no, Inspector,' said Joy, as she stepped out of the front door, taking Macleod by the hand. 'Come in, come in,' she wrapped her arm through his, and almost dragged the Inspector through. Once inside, she stepped behind him, put her hands up to his shoulder, and started taking off his coat. 'It's warm in the house. I don't think you'll be needing that.'

'Thank you,' said Macleod.

'Come through, come through. You don't mind if I continue my workout while we talk?'

'As long as you can talk,' said Macleod.

'Of course,' said Joy, 'I don't think I'm that out of shape,' and she gave a laugh. She took him through to a room at the back of the house where Macleod saw a bike, a mat rolled out, and several weights at the side.

'Do you work out, Inspector?'

'I can't say that I do. I don't get a lot of time with my work.'

'Of course not. I try to stay in shape; do you think it's working?'

Macleod was quite unsure how to take that, but Joy stood in front of him, forcing him to look at her.

'You certainly seem to be in shape. I'm sure you could handle a short run without any problems,' Macleod said dryly.

'Stand over there,' said Joy, and she jumped onto the bike. She started to push hard on the pedals, and once she got into a rhythm, she looked up at Macleod. 'Ask away. Ask away.'

'Well,' said Macleod, 'I've got a couple of things that may not be to your liking. They might touch a sore point, but I need to ask them. My sergeant spoke to Miss Sarah MacIver. I don't know if you are aware that Miranda Folly posed for Sarah for a number of weeks as part of her project at the college. The photographs she took, they were…' Macleod wondered how best to put this, 'nudes. Tasteful, but nudes.'

'Well, I did know about it,' said Sarah. 'I overheard them. Disgusting, really, don't you think? A woman parading herself like that?'

Macleod stared at the woman in front of him. He wasn't sure that you rode a bike in that particular shape, but every angle she seemed to present, he reckoned, was an attempt to lure him, to get him to look at different parts of her. Macleod turned away and looked out the window.

'Sarah said you came to her. Tried to get her to take photographs of you. Said you wanted to be in Miranda's place.'

'I don't think that's quite how it was,' said Joy. 'I think you'll find that the girl needed someone, and I said I was available.'

159

'That's not what she said. She was making the deal with Miranda when you jumped in. She said that you would pose however.'

'You think that of me, Inspector, or is that just your mind working overtime?'

Macleod kept looking out the window. 'I'm not here to think something of people,' he said, 'I'm here to find out what happened and why. Why did you make the offer? Were you jealous of Miranda Folly?'

'Why would I be jealous of that? She was offering to do those disgusting photographs. I wasn't. I said I would pose, obviously, something nice. In good clothing? Yes. Obviously, I wanted to look sexy, but not vulgar like that. That's not me, Inspector. Surely, you don't think that of me.' Macleod heard the bike stop, Joy breathing deeply. He turned to see the woman step off, sweat pouring from her face. 'I don't need to attract men like that, do I?' she said.

'I couldn't comment on that,' said Macleod. 'What I want to know is then why would Sarah say that?'

'Because I wanted to be paid. Miranda would do it for nothing.'

'But it was a project for the college. She wasn't exactly looking to make money off it herself.'

'A woman shouldn't do things like that without being prepared to be paid,' said Joy haughtily.

'So, you would have done what Miranda did?'

Macleod could see Joy was becoming angry.

'I would have probably agreed to something like that in the end, but it would've been much more civilized. I wouldn't have just flaunted myself.'

'Something else Sarah said, and she's not been the only one.

160

A number of other people have witnessed this in the coffee club.'

"What?" asked Joy. She had climbed off the bike and was now standing with her hands on her hips in front of Macleod.

'Well, she said you had a thing for Donald MacDonald. Is that correct?'

'Donald and I have known each other for a long time.'

"I know what a long time is here. I know we have our reunions from school after twenty, thirty, forty, fifty years, and on, where we all know each other, and we're all close,' said Macleod. 'That's not what I'm talking about. Were you closer than that? Did you want to be closer than that?'

'Donald was married,' said Joy. 'I'm not that sort of woman.'

'Were you jealous of Miranda?'

'Why?'

'Well, because of her attentions from Donald. Everyone said he was all eyes for her.'

'All eyes is one thing. Donald was married. That's not something I would get in the way of. I've told you, Inspector, I come from the church like yourself. You should know that. I think we're more akin than these people you're investigating.' With that, Joy seemed to calm down. She walked over to Macleod, putting her arm around him, up on his shoulder. 'Come, let's have a drink in the kitchen.' Macleod felt himself being forced through the door. He was plunked down on a stool. 'I'm going to have a smoothie. Would you like one?'

'I'm afraid I'm not much of a man for drinking my fruit,' said Macleod. 'You can make me a coffee if you want.'

'Of course, Inspector,' said Joy, and immediately went over to start up the kettle. Macleod almost laughed inside. *If she knew anything about me, she'd know one way to scare me off is*

161

*to make an instant coffee.* He watched as the woman made her way over to the fridge, took out her smoothie, poured it, and placed her glass directly opposite him.

In returning to the kettle, she fixed his black coffee, placed it in front of him, then stood, but with elbows down on the table, her face, less than five inches from his. From where he was looking, she was clearly trying to show more than just a good smile.

Macleod started to feel awkward. *You really shouldn't.* A part of him actually liked this woman if she would stop being overbearing. She was bubbly like Jane, but unlike Jane, she didn't seem to have any wisdom. He also had a soft spot at the moment because he felt she was being victimised, made out to be something she wasn't, but he had to go through the motions; he had to make sure that he wasn't missing something.

'I think you were in love with Donald MacDonald. I don't think he returned that in any way.'

'What makes you think that?' asked Joy, now standing up, arms folded in a much more defensive posture.

'From the people I've interviewed, when they talk about you. They say that you constantly noticed the attentions of Donald to Miranda, the eyes, and you kept stepping in the way. You kept trying to take Donald's attention. Then we find out that Miranda goes to pose provocatively. You step in there. I do think you are a woman of the book in a lot of ways, or you think you are. I think you try to do your best, but I also think that you're lonely. I know what it is to be lonely," said Macleod. 'I lost my wife a long time ago. Until my recent partner, I could probably identify with you, albeit I showed it in a very different way.'

'I'm not lonely, Inspector. You make me sound like some

sort of desperate woman.'

'I think you are desperate for something,' said Macleod. 'Desperate to be the centre of somebody's world. It's not a bad thing. It's sad that you haven't found that person. Part of me doesn't understand why, but I do believe that it made you jealous of Miranda Folly.'

Joy Grundy's face became red, even more red than when she'd been on the bike. 'Measure your words carefully, Inspector.'

'I don't know if you felt strong enough to take action. I don't know if Donald's lack of attention slighted you. They do say a woman scorned, don't they?'

Joy stared at him, and Macleod could feel the anger rising inside her.

'I also think that you volunteered to do those photographs against your better judgment. I think, normally, you wouldn't have even entertained the idea of something like that. Oh, yes. I think you would've quite happily posed for photographs, all your clothes on, looking well, but to go further than that, to go to that type of more erotic picture, I think that was driven by your desire to be ahead of Miranda.'

"Are you accusing me of killing her?"

"No,' said Macleod,' but you're also lying to me.'

"Get out,' said Joy. 'Get out.'

'Just for the record, said Macleod, 'have you ever used thallium?'

"Get out!" shouted Joy.

'For the record,' said Macleod. 'Did you kill Miranda Folly and Donald MacDonald? Did you kill Counsellor Morgan? Did you attempt to kill Annie Spence?'

"No,' said Joy. 'Now, get out,' she marched round the table, grabbed Macleod's shoulder, pulling him. He didn't struggle back, but simply stood up as she then marched down the hallway, re-entered the kitchen with his coat, and flung it at him.

'I thought you were something; you seemed like a decent man, but you said such things about me. Just get out.'

"Thank you for your time,' said Macleod.

'I am not some desperate woman!'

'Of course not,' said Macleod, but he knew he didn't sound convincing. Inside, that's exactly what he thought she was. He walked to the door, opened it, and looked back. Joy Grundy was standing, arms folded, face like thunder. She marched up the hall.

'Out!'

Macleod stepped out to the front door, barely getting his foot out in time before it was slammed behind him. Rather than walk away, he stood and listened.

She must have sat down behind the door before he heard her start to cry. He knew now that she didn't do it, but he also knew that she wasn't the only woman to be desperate. Desperate for someone, but she was no killer. The women on the team had been right. She would tell him more than everybody else, even if she hadn't used words. He returned to the car, feeling a lot worse than when he arrived.

# Chapter 19

Macleod felt he needed to check out what had gone on between Joy Grundy and Councillor Morgan from the other side of the equation. Unfortunately, Councillor Morgan was dead so he decided to head to the next best source, that being his wife. The hour was now getting late, and when Hope joined him, Macleod was happy to see a smiling face.

'How did it go with Joy Grundy?' asked Hope.

'I got what I needed.'

'Well, that sounds particularly cryptic.'

'It wasn't the most pleasant experience.'

The car went into silence as they drove through the streets of Stornoway. The dark night was lit up by some streetlights and as they passed by Bayhead and the playpark area, Macleod could see lights set into the trees, making the street seem somewhat brighter and more appealing.

'Are you going to tell me about it?' asked Hope.

'Probably not. After all, I did find out what we all thought.'

'That being?'

'She didn't do it. I'm convinced of it. She didn't do it.'

'Okay,' said Hope. 'I know we all thought she didn't do it,

but the thing that we didn't have was evidence. I know your gut tells you one thing at times, Seoras, but we still have to back it up.'

'Everything's pointing at her, isn't it? Everybody else is squeaky clean.'

'Except for this gun club thing.'

'Well, yes. Innes Stewart is tagged in with that, but he's not done anything about the decision made. It's all very random. And suddenly all these other people have died. If Innes Stewart was annoyed at his gun club being attacked, why would he have taken out Councillor Morgan and Donald MacDonald and Miranda Folly. Why? He would've gone for Joy Grundy. No, this all flashes back to Grundy again. She was humiliated. She doesn't take humiliation well.'

'Did you humiliate her?' asked Hope.

'No,' said Seoras, and then he stopped. 'Certainly not intentionally. She may have had a home truth.'

'What happened?' asked Hope. Macleod relayed his time at Joy Grundy's and how she'd reacted against him.

'From what you said, I think you've called it right,' said Hope. 'You could have been a little bit more subtle about it.'

'Yes,' said Macleod, 'but I needed to know for sure. I needed to get confirmation that that's the type of woman she was. She fell apart. I mean, I'm sorry; I'm all but a married man. I have a stable partner. I told her about that and yet she still seemed to come after me.'

'People do,' said Hope. 'These things happen.'

'I'm afraid they don't happen to me very often. I know people do become fond of people,' he said looking at Hope. 'For a while, I was very fond of you.'

'Whoa,' said Hope. 'Like I didn't know that. I'm still fond of

166

you,' she said.

'Yes,' said Macleod, 'but we are fond of each other but not in that way, not in the way Joy Grundy was showing.'

'That's not fondness,' said Hope. 'There's more beyond that. You said yourself, she wants to be at the front of it. She wants to be the attention. She's seeking love. She's not giving it.'

'True,' said Macleod. 'It's just a sad state of affairs. Sorry, I think she got to me underneath it. I think in there, there's a decent woman.'

Hope turned the corner in the car, pulled over and stopped. 'Look, Seoras, she probably is, but it's not your problem. You didn't cause this situation. Lots of other people did and it's brought it to a head. I've just got you back from stopping feeling self-pity about these blessed newspaper reporters. Don't go off on me just because some woman tried to turn your head.'

'It's funny sometimes,' said Macleod. 'You can sound like Jane.'

Hope punched him. 'Don't ever tell her that. Now, get your head on. Let's see if we can clear up what happened in this Council Chamber.'

Macleod nodded, but Hope noticed he was still quite sombre as they drove along. Arriving at a large five-bedroom house on the outskirts of Stornoway, Macleod rang the doorbell which chimed loudly. The door was opened by a tall woman, with brunette hair, but whose eyes were deep-set and red. She'd clearly been crying and was dressed in a pair of jeans and a large jumper.

'Sorry to disturb you, ma'am. One of our sergeants called round previously advising you about your husband. I'm DI Macleod, and this is DS McGrath. We're investigating your

167

husband's death along with those of other people he associated with at the Cortado Club. Would it be possible to come in and have a word?'

Macleod pulled out his credentials, but the woman wasn't looking and waved them away. Hope looked at Macleod, raising her eyebrow somewhat, and they followed the woman through to the lounge.

'Can I make you a cup of coffee or something, Inspector?' the woman asked.

'No. You don't need to go to that trouble.' And he sat down on a long sofa with Hope. The woman sat in a chair before a small stove that seemed to blast out enough heat to power a steam engine.

'I haven't really moved much in the last day or two,' she said. 'I can't believe he's gone.'

'I'm deeply sorry for your loss,' said Macleod, 'but there's an incident I've come across that might be relevant to our case. Unfortunately, your husband isn't here to talk about it, and I just wanted to see if he had mentioned it to you.'

'What incident?'

'Well, your husband, he was a councillor, and at one point, the gun club was up for trying to renew their licence to operate down in Harris. I believe the council made a vote on it. It said that your husband had some opposition from one Joy Grundy. Do you know Miss Grundy?'

'Oh, I know Miss Grundy,' said the woman. 'I think a lot of women with husbands know Miss Grundy. She has that image, doesn't she? The church background, but really she's a flirt.'

'Okay,' said Macleod, 'but I was thinking more specifically about that particular instance. Do you know what happened?

168

Did your husband speak about it?'

'Well,' she said, 'I knew it was coming up and I asked him how it was going. He said that Joy Grundy had taken him aside, actually took him for lunch to talk about it. She saw him as the biggest opposition to refusing the licence because he's quite close to that Innes Stewart. Well, I say he's quite close; my husband was heavily involved in the Island Games and Innes was a bit of a star of his. He reckoned it would bring a lot of good publicity to the island with what he was doing. Joy was about to put a blocker on that and so he was dead keen to get passed.

'But he came back one night and I said to him before he'd gone where was he going and he said it was a business meeting to do with the council. One of the other councillors had asked to take him to dinner to talk about an issue. I thought nothing of it because I thought it would be one of the men but apparently not, it was Joy Grundy. And she took him for a late-night meal, all quaint with a candle and that. He came back telling me he was reconsidering. And I said, "Why?" Are you married, Inspector?'

'Yes.'

Hope looked at Macleod out of the corner and eye, and he simply gave a nod to her.

'Well, you'll understand then,' said Mrs Morgan. 'You trust each other, but you can tell when things affect you. Joy Grundy had got through to my husband. He always had a roving eye, but he was faithful. He was a good man, but he liked to look. Wasn't anything weird, just when we were out and about, I could tell, but he never roved away from home, so that was fine. It wasn't like he didn't look at me as well, but she took him for a candle-lit meal. And when he came back, his mind

169

wasn't with me. It was elsewhere.'

'So, what did you do from there?' asked Hope.

'I fought for him,' she said. 'It's what you do. Isn't that right, inspector?' Macleod nodded. 'You see, the whole thing was about her enticing him to get him round to her way of thinking on the gun club. I have to say I gave him hell. I said to him, "You're a councillor. You represent people. You stand for people. If this doesn't go through, think about Innes, think about what's not going to happen." You see, he wasn't thinking with his brain. He was thinking, well, you know what with.'

Macleod gave a cough as if the comment was a little too much but Hope simply nodded. 'How did he respond to that?' asked Hope.

'It doesn't take me long to get my husband back on side,' said the woman, but tears started to fall from her eyes. 'At least it didn't. I won't be able to get him back on my side anymore. Oh, he went out all guns blazing, Sergeant. He went for her in the chamber that night. I don't know if he was happy doing it, but he did it for me. I told him what was needed. Sometimes I had to do that with him. He was a good man. He wanted to do his best for this place, this island, but there's a lot of intricacies about how you work here. A lot of people firmly entrenched.'

'I'm very aware of that,' said Macleod.

'He wasn't that fixed himself, but if you don't stand up on certain things, you certainly won't get elected.'

'And he stood from a church background, didn't he?' said Macleod. 'I believe his manifesto for the council election said so, half of it, according to my constable, based on that.'

'You understand how it is though, Inspector. He had to get elected. That's how we did it.'

'So, you basically worked him up to attack her?' said Hope.

'Verbally, in a professional sense, yes,' said the woman, suddenly becoming animated. 'That bitch tried to take my husband. Do you understand me? She tried to take him. You don't do that. She deserved everything coming to her. I saw her the days before the vote, the day before the debate, and she was there trying to come up to talk to him. She was all over him, the perfume, everything. It made me angry, and I went for her.'

'You never thought she was just pleading her cause, trying to work things, as they say?' Hope raised her eyebrows, trying to see if the woman could see from the other side.

'You don't do that. You don't tolerate that sort of behaviour.'

'But as a single woman, maybe that's how she would work. Maybe she didn't understand how far she was going.'

'She knew. She damn well knew. I'm just disappointed that someone would make her the head of their campaign. Hapless idiots never understanding how dangerous she was.'

'Okay,' said Macleod. 'I think we understand how you feel.'

The woman turned, suddenly stood up, coming towards Macleod. 'You understand how I feel, do you think? He's dead. Somebody has just killed him. Did she do it? Tell me, did she do it? My husband used to talk about Miranda. Oh yes, he said she was turning people's heads, and I knew who he meant. He meant Donald, but she turned his head as well. Was she competition in there? Is that what this is all about? Is that why they're all dead? Is this Joy Grundy?'

'Why do you say that?' asked Macleod.

'Because that's what she's like, isn't it? You hear things, and I saw them first hand, but she's more than that.'

'Who said it?' asked Macleod.

'Everyone. People I talk to. Donald's family have been over

171

as well; they confirm it. Going after a man like that, a good family man, and my husband, a councillor, decent, upstanding man.'

'Every man's human,' said Hope.

'Indeed,' said the woman, 'and they can have their head turned by the way these women behave. They shouldn't be here; they should get out. Try to work a decent life. Look what happens. Did she do it, Inspector? Did she kill him because she couldn't have him? Did she do it because she felt humiliated?'

Macleod stood up. 'Did he humiliate her? Did he have to?'

'She deserved everything she got.' The woman turned away and made her way back to the fire. 'Was there anything else, Inspector, because you've really brought up some bad memories?'

'No. Thank you,' said Macleod. 'We'll see ourselves out.'

'Sir,' said Hope, 'don't you?'

'No, Sergeant, we don't. Follow me.' Macleod opened the living room door, made his way out to the driveway and back to the car.

Once inside, Hope turned to face him. 'Surely, there was more to ask there. More antagonism.'

'No,' said Macleod. 'We're getting sent down the rabbit warren here. Everything she said, "people have said", always "people have said". Somebody's behind this. Somebody's stirring things.'

And in his head, all he could hear was, 'Macleod. Macleod. Do you know who did it, Macleod?'

# Chapter 20

The next morning Hope was up early, making her way to the hospital, determined to get there before Annie Spence discharged herself. The woman's recovery was remarkable, and Hope thought that the killer must have missed by a long way while trying to drop the thallium into her cup. Maybe they got disturbed but it was a sleight of hand that didn't seem to marry with the three successful attempts before.

The day was bright and cold and as Hope walked through the front entrance of the Western Isles Hospital, she found herself enjoying time alone. The previous night had been difficult with Macleod, and she knew her boss was feeling quite emotional about the case. Hopefully, he'd spoken to his better half in the later night. She knew Jane had such a way of bringing the man round.

Hope strode along to Annie Spence's ward where she spoke briefly to the nurse, who advised that Annie was getting changed at that time. Hope took a seat in the corridor, waiting, and then Annie Spence appeared. The woman seemed to hobble out, her back slightly arched but Hope noticed the determined face. The woman picked up her bag and as she moved along, Hope intercepted her.

'Miss Spence.'

'Yes.'

'I'm Detective Sergeant Hope McGrath. I'm here to give you a lift back. The doctors may have mentioned it last night.'

'Good. Why don't you get my bag? I don't think we've met before.'

'No, we haven't,' said Hope. 'I tried to meet you. In fact, I spoke to you at the door but you weren't for opening.'

'I didn't see your card.'

Hope removed her credentials from inside her leather jacket and showed them quickly to Annie before putting them back.

'Make yourself useful,' said Annie. 'Take my bag.' Hope picked the bag up, wondering if the neighbour had dropped the items in when she realised it was quite heavy.

'Are we taking something home from the hospital in here?' asked Hope. Annie ignored her, shuffling her way along the corridor, leaving Hope in her wake. 'The car's outside at the front,' said Hope. 'Do you want me to get one of the staff to bring the wheelchair?'

'I told that doctor I'm fine—now enough. Just bring the bag.'

*Charming*, thought Hope. The woman really had endeared herself to Hope but the Glaswegian-born detective decided it was just the woman's way, so quietly followed her along the corridors and out to the front of the hospital. When they reached the outside, Annie turned on her, almost fiercely. 'Where's your car?'

'It's out in the car park,' said Hope.

'Are you expecting me to walk all the way down there?'

'No,' said Hope. 'I expect you to stand here while I bring the car over.'

'Well, get on with it then. That's the trouble with young people; they're not considerate.'

Hope wondered if the woman was being deliberately antagonistic, and she certainly seemed wrapped up in her own thoughts.

'What are you desperate to get home for?' said Hope when she pulled up in the car and opened the door. 'Do you like those daytime programs?'

'I thought Macleod would come and pick me up. That would be better, wouldn't it? Macleod, he'd have a real concern, understand old people better.'

'He is closer to your age,' said Hope, doing her best to take no offense at the woman. 'Your neighbour said you liked those TV programs featuring detectives. Is that right?'

'What I watch is my own business,' said Annie. She closed the door of the car and put her seatbelt on. 'Take me home.'

'No problem,' said Hope, starting the car. 'The boss said you liked those TV programs too. What do you watch? The American ones?'

'I don't like the American ones,' said Annie. 'It's not proper, is it? It's not real. It's not Macleod. I've seen Macleod on the telly.'

'Indeed,' said Hope. 'We've been on a few times lately. We were on that boat.'

'The boat on the River Ness. I saw that. Well, I saw Macleod. Don't think you had much to do with it, did you?'

Hope thought back to the previous case with what could only be described as a madman who started butchering supposed wrongdoers. They'd ended up on a boat in the middle of the River Ness and Hope had dived into the water to save a man.

*No*, she thought, *I didn't do much. I was in trouble being in the shadow of Macleod. It was always his team, always the things that he did. Sometime she'd have to get out, make a name for herself. It didn't matter if she was mentioned to other people up above. She needed her own team to solve her own cases. Then she'd be fine.*

In the meantime, Hope didn't really care. She was more interested in getting back to John in Inverness, the man who was currently lighting up her life. *Times were good*, she thought. *Even this old birdie can't spoil that.*

They pulled up on the street in front of Annie Spence's house and Hope got out, walking around the car before opening the door for Annie Spence.

'I'm not a cripple. I can do it myself. Get the bag.' Hope shrugged her shoulders, looked in the boot, and took Annie's bag out. By this stage, the woman had made it all the way to the door, opened it, and closed it behind her. Hope banged on the door. There was no reply. She banged on it two times, then a third. It slowly crept opened.

'You haven't got your bag, Ms. Spence.' The door opened more fully, and Hope stepped through with the bag.

'That's fine. You've seen me in. I should probably say thanks for getting the bag. You can go now. I'm home safely, see.'

Hope wondered how she should play this.

'The thing is, Annie, Macleod says I should stay for a bit, make sure you're all right. He wanted me to talk through a few safety tips considering we've got a killer on the loose. Is that all right?'

The woman seemed to grumble and then she walked off into the kitchen. Hope carried the bag through to the living room where she saw an old sofa along with a Parker Knoll chair. She recognised the type. They were good quality when sitting was difficult, something thankfully she hadn't experienced yet.

Hope saw the net curtains and realised that you couldn't really see out from this side either.

A few minutes later, Annie trotted into the living room, plunked herself down in the Parker Knoll chair with a cup of tea in her hand, and switched on the television with the remote. Hope saw the start of one of the BBC's crime dramas.

'Bet you thought you'd never get such excitement here,' said Hope, 'A real drama on your doorstep.'

'Joy Grundy. She's had it, hasn't she? I think that's what Macleod wanted me to say. I think that's what he's suspecting. She seems to be in the middle of everything. You sit in that coffee shop, you hear everything. Everything going on, and Joy Grundy, she's like you, isn't she?'

'Like me?' queried Hope. 'How do you mean?'

'In my day,' said Annie, 'someone like you would be dressed a lot more demurely. Look at you. Those jeans are tight to your backside, love. As for that top, in my day, you wore them a lot looser. You didn't want to show off your curves. You girls today, all curves. I bet that hair of yours is dyed.'

Hope nearly bet at that point but she stopped herself. 'I'm sorry my clothing choices don't get your appreciation, Annie, but the hair is genuine. Those people who test me usually find out it is genuine.'

'What do you mean?'

'Redheads have a temper,' said Hope. 'You don't ignite them.'

Annie gave a tut, picked up her cup of tea, and began to drink some more. She ignored Hope and stared at the TV screen. Hope looked around the room and could see through an opening in the wall into the dining room behind.

She made her way over for a better look, interested by some pictures on the wall. Annie didn't seem to be taking any

177

interest, so Hope entered the dining room. Looking at the wall, she could see Harry Houdini on an old poster advertising his show. There were plenty of other magicians as well and some of the prints were signed.

She got closer looking at the dates of the signatures but most of them were before the year 2000. She wondered if Annie ever worked any of the shows, but her photo wasn't anywhere amongst them. She glanced further round the room, looking to see if Annie's photo was anywhere, but there were none of her.

There were no photos of children or parents either, just the magicians. She turned and edged around the dining room table. On the sideboard, there were a number of fancy trays but there were also some photographic albums. She took one of them, her eye looking through the hole in the wall to see that Annie was still engrossed in her detective programme.

Hope fully opened the photo album before her and was shocked to see Macleod looking back at her. He wasn't smiling. It was one of those caught in the street shots. Hope recognised the start of her head, which had been cut out of the photograph. If she remembered right, the image was from when he was back here, on that first case, when she'd only just got to know him. They were not such good colleagues then. Hope flipped over a page in the photo book and she saw a photo of herself on the Black Isle. She was in the background, Macleod again in the foreground.

*That was just above Cromarty*, she thought. The second major case they'd taken. There was a further press cutting, about a stay at an estate home on Harris. Then there was the Barra case. Then there was the shooting. The next was from the Fort Augustus attack. Hope continued looking through time and again. There was all the Santa Clauses that died. A photo of Macleod near the Kessock Bridge where one of them had jumped. A note stated that D.I. Macleod had tried to prevent it.

No wonder the woman kept asking for him. She was obviously a big fan. Hope made it to the end of the book and the woman still hadn't looked around. She walked over to the window, looked out to the back garden and she saw a small row of flowers around the cut lawn. Hope didn't know what the flowers were, but each one looked the same.

She stared down. She thought that the soil was disturbed around some of them. *Maybe she goes out and pots them every night again*, thought Hope. Hope returned to the front room where the program was still in full swing, probably no more than halfway through.

'You knew about the gun club issue, didn't you?'

'Macleod tell you that? It's good he's recognised his limits in this. I like Macleod, but he needs help. He doesn't know everything; sometimes he acts like he does, but he doesn't know everything.'

'Inspector Macleod never thinks he knows everything. When we come to a case, we don't know anything. That's when we start looking.'

'He sees things; he's not like you,' said Annie. 'I know why you're there, just someone to make the force look good. Hey, look, we're now employing attractive women. Look at you, you don't even have to wear a skirt, and a proper skirt at that. No, you'll get to swan around in your jeans. Looks like they've been painted on you. Let the men talk to you, though, don't they? I bet you flash your eyes at them. Make sure you've got that tight clothing on when you talk to them.'

Hope restrained herself. She reckoned there was no point even trying to give a come back here. In fact, she felt like she was being wound-up.

'He's got to have somebody good looking on his arm, hasn't he?

'Who?' asked the woman.

'Macleod,' said Hope. 'Younger girl on his arm. That's what happens in these detective things, isn't it?'

'Not now,' said Annie. 'In the sixties, yes. You had the man doing the detecting, the woman on his arm. Not now. They have all sorts of women run some of these shows. What's the point of that?' Hope thought this woman was the worst advocate for feminism she'd ever had. 'Some of the men aren't even men in this.'

'It's a different day, Annie.'

'Too right, it is,' she said. 'Too right. I need more men like Macleod; he can solve anything if he puts his mind to it. He's like the pilot, isn't he?' She said that looking at Hope. 'You're the trolley dolly.'

Hope kept her face perfectly still because she felt the woman was never going to let up. She wasn't going to let herself be pulled in. Her hand moved up to the scar that run across her face, suffered when she prevented an acid attack.

*I'm Macleod's partner!* She never thought of herself as a trolley dolly and what an old-fashioned term as well. Hope only laughed. 'Don't open the door to anyone, Annie,' said Hope, 'but I guess you know that anyway. You certainly didn't open it to me.'

'I'm watching my programmes. You've done the lift. You can tell Macleod you've been a good little girl. Now, off you go.'

*Cheeky cow*, thought Hope. *How does she get away with it?*

But Hope also thought there was no chance of changing the woman's mind. *Detectives and magicians,* she thought. *What a combination and not a single woman on the wall. She really was old school.*

'By the way,' said Annie suddenly, 'you can tell Macleod, and make sure you take this message properly—you might want to write it down. Tell him that the gun club issue, she put people on the edge. Joy Grundy was a woman who always wanted her way, and she didn't get it that time. He probably wants to look at Joy Grundy. Told him that. Don't come next time.'

'I'm sorry?'

'I said don't come next time. I want Macleod. Next time, tell Macleod to come. I've got more for Macleod.'

'Well, it's been a joy,' said Hope. 'Long live the revolution.'

'What?' said Annie, apparently unable to hear.

'I said, next time I'll send Macleod,' said Hope. And the woman nodded and turned back to her TV. Hope made for the front door, opened it, and sat down in the car. *Damn right,* she thought. *Next time I'm sending Macleod. I'd send Ross, but God help him. Who knows what he'd get?*

# Chapter 21

Hope McGrath climbed the steps to the upper floor of Stornoway Police Station and made her way along the corridor to find the room that the murder investigation team was working in. Macleod was at the head of the room, sitting behind his desk, looking through some reports in front of him. As Hope entered the room, she got a nod from Ross and then Clarissa but didn't talk to her subordinates. She felt she needed to talk to Macleod first.

'Annie home?' he asked.

'Yes, Seoras, and even got inside the building today.'

'Really? Was that interesting?'

'Well, actually, it was. Let me grab a coffee.'

Macleod handed his cup over. 'Get me one, too,' he said.

Hope almost rolled her eyes, but took his cup across to the far side of the room. Having poured coffee from the ever-ready filter machine, she came back and placed his cup in front of him and pulled up a seat at Macleod's side of the desk.

'All okay?' he said.

'I don't know,' said Hope. 'I took her home and well, you know what she's like. Obstinate woman seems to think that my generation has nothing, but she certainly likes you.'

'Oh, don't get started,' said Macleod. 'All the time, Macleod, when I saw her, over and over.'

'Yes. She never calls you Inspector, does she? Never calls you anything except Macleod. And she says it in that fashion.'

'But she's from the island.'

'I know,' said Hope, 'but more than that, when I took her in, she sat down and it seems that all she watches is lots of daytime television—and detectives. Lots of detectives.'

'I don't think that's unusual. Woman's lonely on her own, doesn't really mean much.'

'No, Seoras, it doesn't. Except I went through into her dining room and then I saw on the wall, magicians, Houdini on the old posters of his show adorning a wall quite out of the blue. I mean, the living room had nothing like that. Normal sort of knickknacks you'd see in a house, but the dining room, full of magicians.'

'Obviously, she likes her magic, Hope,' said Macleod.

'But more than that, she had a photograph album. I opened it and she's got pictures of you.'

'Of me?'

'Of you. Press clippings, all those images you see when you get screenshotted in the paper. In one, we are half walking away and half your head's cut off in this because it didn't quite grab your photograph correctly, but all the photographs are of you. I'm there occasionally in the background. There's background cameos from Ross, Clarissa, even Kirsten from back in the day.'

'Back in the day? How far back does this go?'

'When we started working together. The first case down here, the press cutting that had a story about us being in the water with the body in the bag, trying to keep her afloat.'

In their first case, it had come down to a battle in the elements at Holm on the Isle of Lewis. The murder suspect, her son, and another victim wrapped up in a bag had entered the water and Macleod and Hope had gone in after them. Hope saved the day and had given Macleod a ring to float with, but she had held the victim up in the cold water until the RNLI lifeboat had arrived. The murderer and her son were never seen again, but the story had made the press all over the island and through much in the mainland.

'So, she has the story of the attempted shooting at Fort Augustus. And more, Seoras, even the murders up north right through, she quoted me something. That's right, she talked about you being on the telly. I think the woman's obsessed with you. I mean, the way she says 'Macleod' all the time, absolutely obsessed.'

Macleod sat back and Hope let him be because she could tell the mind was working.

'You don't think,' said Macleod.

'What?' said Hope.

'She's significantly older, isn't she?'

'Well, she certainly shuffled along when I took her home,' said Hope.

Macleod sat back again and Hope was on edge, desperate to find out where his mind was going.

'Seoras,' the voice came from across the room.

'Don't bother him at the moment. He's in the middle of thinking something through,' said Hope.

'Inspector,' retorted Clarissa, 'Joy Grundy is missing. It appears she was grabbed.'

Macleod instantly sat up. 'What do you mean, grabbed?'

'It's just come from downstairs. She was walking along the

street to meet a friend. The friend saw her from a distance; she was pulled into a red car.'

'Red car? Red car,' said Macleod. 'When we went to visit Mrs Morgan, she had a red car in her drive. I'm sure of it.'

'She did,' said Hope. 'She blooming well did.'

Macleod stood up, moving across for his coat. 'Hope, you're with me. Clarissa and Ross, stay here, coordinate. I want an island-wide search for her. Call on the other agencies, if necessary. In fact, no, just do it. We don't want to be behind the curve on this one.'

'Where do we look?'

'Clarissa, talk to the friend. We're looking for red cars, anything like that, particularly, get a better description of it. She may even have got a partial plate. See if she's any idea of what the people look like that took Grundy. People on the street, ask around. Get moving on that. I'm going on a hunch that she's up at the Morgan's, but you go through the processes.'

'Will do,' said Clarissa. Macleod heard her pick up the phone, utter the words 'Sergeant Doolin'. Hope was behind Macleod, pulling on her leather jacket and ran down the corridor after him.

'Morgan, you think?'

'I don't think she did it herself. She's not capable, not of that grab in the street, but she might know who did. She might have set them up to it.'

Hope followed her boss down the stairs, out into the car park, and pressed the button for the car, allowing Macleod to get into the passenger seat. Hope tore through the town in the car, making their way up to Counselor Morgan's house, where they saw a red car parked outside. As soon as Hope stopped the car, Macleod was out, running down the driveway, up to the front door. He rang the bell and banged on the door, almost simultaneously, and Hope caught up with him just as the door opened. Mrs Morgan stood there, looking rather incensed.

'What the blazes is up with you?'

'Don't mess me about. I want to know if you know the whereabouts of Joy Grundy.'

'I wouldn't know Joy Grundy's location any more than anyone else. Why would I? I don't want to see that woman, little witch.'

'I said, don't mess me about.'

'I have nothing to say, Inspector, and you can't come here like this, charging around. I have rights, you know.'

'At the moment, you are a suspect in a possible kidnapping. If you want, we'll do this down the station, but I really haven't got time. Where is she?'

'I haven't seen Joy Grundy in weeks. I don't go near that woman.'

Hope could see Macleod staring, his eyes fixed, and the woman began to shake.

'If they've taken her and you know about it, you're an accessory. They kill her, it's murder. You really want that? For all that you hate the woman, I don't think you're the murdering type.'

'I really don't know what you're talking about, Inspector. Now, that's enough,' and she swung the door, trying to close it, but Macleod put his foot in the gap.

'That's a form of assault, Inspector.'

'McGrath, read her rights. We're taking her in.'

The woman's face changed completely. 'I can come down and speak to you at the station, if you wish.'

'Oh, no. You come now, right now. Right now!' bellowed Macleod.

'Inspector, this is not on. I said I'll cooperate. Let me go and sort my hair out and I'll be along in an hour.'

At the top of his voice, Macleod shouted, 'She doesn't have an hour.' Hope wondered what he was doing. It wasn't Macleod's way, but she heard him again shout even louder, 'If she's dead, you'll be the one up for it.'

Hope was suddenly aware that several neighbours had poked their heads out of their doors. Some were coming over to see what the commotion was.

'Are you all right, Mrs Morgan?' said a voice from across the wall.

'Mrs Morgan is helping the police in their inquiries to find Joy Grundy who has disappeared,' said Macleod loudly. 'Kindly don't interfere. She'll be coming down to the station with us to answer some questions.'

Morgan's face sunk. Macleod said under his breath, 'I want to march you right out of here in front of everyone. Let them all see. I don't care that you may not be directly involved; you're withholding information that could save a life. On that basis, I will show you up for what you are to all your neighbours.'

At the top of her voice, Hope said, 'If you'd like to accompany us, Mrs Morgan, we'll just go into the car now.'

'Don't,' said Morgan. 'Don't.' Hope could see the woman beginning to shake.

'Your choice,' said Macleod under his breath.

'The McDonalds have taken her. Donella was around. She asked if I wanted to get involved, come and see her before . . .'

'Before what?' asked Macleod.

'They're going to give her some of her own medicine.'

'You stupid woman,' said Macleod. 'She didn't kill anybody.'

'You think I care about that? She enticed my husband. She made his friend cheat on his wife; she's one of my friends. The woman deserves whatever's happening to her.'

'You have half an hour. There'll be a car here to take you to the station.'

'Sir?' asked Hope.

Macleod turned around. 'The McDonalds. Let's go.' The pair ran for their car, Macleod pulling out his phone. As Hope raced away in the car, Macleod sat in the passenger seat, calling Ross, advising him to send the car to pick up Mrs Morgan.

'A taste of her own medicine, that's what they said.'

'That's right, Hope,' said Macleod. 'I hope we're not going to be too late.'

The car sped through Stornoway, back to the MacDonald's house. Macleod could hear police cars in the distance, the sirens wailing, but hoped he was there first. As he ran up to the door, Hope thought she could see no movement inside. She ran round the back but could see no one in there either.

'Seoras, there's no one home. They're not here.'

'Of course not,' he said. 'You're not going to do it here. Too many witnesses.' He turned and made his way next door, banging on the front door. It took half a minute, but then the door opened, and a man stood in his dressing gown, yawning.

'What the hell's the problem here?'

'Sorry, sir. Detective Inspector Macleod. Do you know your neighbours?'

'The McDonalds? Well, we know her, of course, and the kids, but he's dead.'

'I am aware, sir. How well do you know them?'

'Well, big family. It's not just the ones there, she has brothers and that.'

'Do they have another residence?'

'Well, I'm sure the brothers have their own, but what do you mean?'

'Do they have any other buildings?'

'Hang on a minute,' he said. The man disappeared into the house.

Macleod turned to Hope, 'Hope, phone the station. Get the addresses of all the brothers, sisters, relatives of the McDonalds. Get cars going there, now.'

Hope turned away, picked up the phone, passed a message quickly to Ross. Once she closed down the call, the man had returned in his dressing gown, but with a map in front of him.

'I don't know if this is relevant. I don't know where the brothers and sisters now live, but I know MacDonald told me once that they own a little farm. Well, I don't know if they run it as a farm anymore, but the homestead is out here. They used to go there in the summer, sometimes. It's not a big building, but . . .'

'But nothing, sir. May I take the map?'

'Of course,' he said. 'Not a problem.'

Macleod went to turn away, but then quickly turned back. 'That's the only other building you know of?'

'Yes,' said the man. 'Sorry, I couldn't be more of help beyond.'

'Oh, you've been spectacular,' said Macleod. 'Go back to sleep.' He turned to Hope, 'Let's go. I think I know where they are.'

# Chapter 22

The map had the building marked as a farm and it was located four miles outside Stornoway on the road towards Harris. Hope put the foot down, swerving past cars along the single carriageway road, pushing the car as hard as she could. Macleod had put his hand up, holding onto the handle located just above his door, something he always employed when Hope was driving particularly fast.

'Ross,' shouted Macleod down the phone, 'you need to get out to their farm, four miles out of Stornoway. I've got grid coordinates. Send me some cars there as well, please. I think this is where they are . . . No, keep the others going. We need to cover all bases on this.'

'Clarissa has got the Mountain Rescue, sir, Coastguard search teams on the move as well.'

'Don't stop that, keep that going, direct some towards my location. We may need them in case they moved her from there, keep our options open. Tell the search teams not to approach, to find a police officer first. The family could be violent.'

Macleod closed down the call, hanging onto the handle again as Hope swerved in and out of the traffic. It wasn't that there was a lot of traffic, it was just that to overtake meant taking a risk at bends that normally she would never dare.

'You think they'll be violent?'

'She's got brothers, and they're going to be under pressure. They grabbed her in daylight; they must be insane, or wound up,' said Macleod. 'Somebody's been spinning stories. Somebody's been underneath this, someone you wouldn't see.'

'How do you mean?'

'I think I know what's going on,' he said, 'but it can wait. We need to get Joy Grundy first.'

They arrived at the coordinates on the map and Hope spun the car to the track that led out into moorland. Although it said it was a farm, it was quite clear that there was no arable land around. Maybe they kept sheep in the past, but whatever, Macleod didn't care. Instead, he saw the small building ahead of him. Two floors, maybe four or five rooms inside at most. There were a number of cars there, and as they stepped out of their own, Macleod warned Hope, telling her to be careful.

'We need to get Grundy as soon as,' he said. 'We don't mess about. Morgan said they were giving her a dose of her own medicine. They think she poisoned everyone.'

'So, what? They're going to poison her?'

'We need to find her quick.' Macleod ran up towards the front door, closely followed by Hope, but before he could knock on it, the door opened and before him stood Donella MacDonald, her arms folded, her face almost wild.

'There's no point coming in, Inspector.'

'Where is Joy Grundy?'

'She's not here. You can go through the entire house but she's not here.'

'Whose car is that?' said Macleod, pointing over to a red

one.

'It's my brother's. He's in here.'

'The other car?'

'That's mine,' she said.

'What about the white one beyond it?'

'My other brother.'

'The last one?'

'Donald's sister.'

'They're all in there,' said Macleod, pushing his way past.

'You won't find anything in here, Inspector, I told you.'

'Hope,' said Macleod, 'go upstairs. Check it out.'

Macleod was in a hallway with stairs to his right-hand side. He made his way on through and found a kitchen, passing a woman who was giving him daggers. He searched on into the living room where a fire was blazing. Two men sat on the sofa saying nothing.

'Where is she?' asked Macleod.

'We don't know what you're talking about.' Macleod looked at the man. He could see the resemblance to Donella MacDonald.

'Tell me now. Tell me now or I'll lock you up and throw away the key for murder.'

'We don't know where she is. No idea.'

Macleod looked around but he couldn't see anything. Nothing. No sign of Joy Grundy. Macleod went up the stairs, but he was closely followed by Donella MacDonald.

'There'll be nothing up there as well,' she said. As he approached, he found Hope in one of the bedrooms, throwing the covers off, looking under the bed, then in the wardrobes. She tore off into another room doing the same. They spent the next ten minutes running around, poking at every crevice of the house, but they found nothing.

'You need to tell me where she is,' said Macleod.

'Why should I?' said Donella. 'Do you know what that woman did to me?'

'It doesn't matter,' said Macleod. 'She didn't kill your husband.'

'So you say, but even if she didn't, she took him from me. She and that harlot, Miranda Folly. I can't get to Folly. I guess Grundy finished her off because she wasn't happy with her taking Donald as well. Did you know Joy was always sweet on him? Even back in the day at school.'

'She told me she was amazed that you got him. He was popular, well-liked. You were a safer option.'

'Safer option?' said Donella, her eyes lighting up. 'That bitch took him; she must have slept with him, her and Miranda Folly. Now she's killed him to cover it up. She killed Folly because there was too much competition. Wanted to get to Donald. Maybe he did or maybe he didn't, or maybe he told her to sling her hook after he had his way with her. I really don't care. She needs to pay for killing my Donald. She's come into the family, attacked it.'

"Enough,' said Macleod. 'Where is she?'

'If I knew, I wouldn't tell you.'

Macleod wandered outside where he could hear the sirens of police cars arriving. He looked around and the day was cool and crisp. The temperature couldn't be more than a couple of degrees above freezing, but here in the moorland with the winter sun shining down, there was an incredible beauty. *She wasn't in the house*, thought Macleod. *Did they take her away somewhere else?*

Hope came out behind him. 'Maybe this is all a stage, maybe

she's not here at all. They've enough brothers and sisters across the two families. Aunts, uncles, and everything else. She could be anywhere. The family's closing ranks,' said Hope.

'They are.' Macleod looked in the short distance and he could see a little hut. It was made of concrete with a wooden door.

'What's that?' asked Hope.

'Old shielings,' said Macleod. 'They don't use that these days. They used to sleep in there when they were out in the moor cutting the peats before the days when you could just run out in your car and back. They're used in the summer.'

'Well, if they brought her here, how about leaving her there? It's innocuous, isn't it?'

'Only if they knew we were coming.'

'If Morgan rang them,' said Hope, 'they wouldn't have had that long before we got here. Maybe they had her in the house. Maybe they took her elsewhere. Maybe they took her there first. At least you could take any evidence and put it in there to clear the house. You wouldn't have that long to react.'

'Go,' said Macleod. Hope turned and began running across the moor. Macleod followed but at a walking pace, his mind elsewhere.

Hope approached the shieling and found a door that had a padlock on it. She noticed that the hook in which the padlock sat was old and rusted, but the padlock itself was new. It was one of those with a simple code, but Hope wasn't for messing about. She turned and legged it. Macleod watched her go past.

'Where are you going?' he shouted after her.

'Back in a minute,' came the reply. Macleod arrived at the shieling just as Hope returned out of breath. He watched his partner bend down with a pair of bolt cutters, setting them

194

around the lock, and then she pushed hard with everything she had. It took three goes but eventually there was a snip.

'Good job they didn't use a proper lock,' said Hope. She worked at the padlock and then threw it away to one side. Quickly, she pulled open the door. Macleod took out his pen torch from inside his coat and started flashing it around inside. He saw some peat stacked up in a corner.

'You don't put peat in here, do you?' said Hope. 'I thought you said it was where they slept.'

'No, you don't,' said Macleod. 'Clear that away.' Hope dived into the stack, quickly throwing the peat out of the way until Macleod's light shone on something yellow. Hope reached in, pulled hard, and eventually, a jacket came loose.

'It's Joy Grundy's,' said Macleod. 'She wore a yellow jacket like that, I'm sure.'

'I think you're right.'

Quickly, Hope checked the pockets and found inside one a loyalty card for a local supermarket. 'It is Joy Grundy's,' she said, putting the jacket down, aware that it could be evidence.

'So they were here; she was here,' said Macleod.

Hope reached in and started to dig away more of the peat. She saw other pieces of material and pulled them out. In the next two minutes, she reckoned she had everything that Joy Grundy would've been wearing, sat before them inside the shieling.

'She can't have anything on,' said Macleod. 'If she was here and she's not in the house, and she's not in here . . .'

'I'm assuming that they didn't have enough time to kill her and bury her,' said Hope. 'Then she must be . . .'

Macleod nodded, 'Right on the moor. They've dumped her somewhere on the moor.' Macleod marched out of the shielings and saw an officer making his way towards him. The young woman stopped.

'Detective Inspector, what do you need from us?'

'Have you got any search teams yet? They should be coming here. Ross said they were coming.'

'I believe so. What are we looking for?'

'Back in that shieling,' he said, 'I found all of Joy Grundy's clothes. I think they've got her out here on the moor somewhere. She's going to have nothing on. They may have done other things to her. I don't think we'll find her in a good way, but we need to find her and quick, because if she's still alive, she may not be for long.'

The officer turned and ran back towards the police cars. Macleod looked beyond them, and he could see one of the dark blue vans from the Coastguard. There was a white 4x4 beside it as well. *One of their newer vehicles*, he thought. Mountain Rescue were behind them.

He turned to Hope, 'Get involved with them and get out onto that moor. See if we can find her. I'm putting the rest of this lot under arrest.' Macleod marched back over to the house and summoned several officers to join him.

The family were sitting in the living room around the fire and Macleod marched into the middle of it, staring at them all.

'We found her clothes. You'll all go down for this. Officers, read them their rights and arrest them, but before you go,' he said to the family sitting down, 'tell me now where she is; tell me where to find her. It'll work in your favour.'

Donella MacDonald stood up, came close to Macleod, and looked him right in the eye. 'Go to hell, Inspector. Go to hell. When you find her, make sure the press get a photograph.

Make sure they understand what a little slut she was. You don't touch this family. She's as she deserves to be, and I hope the whole world sees her. If she's still alive when you find her, tell her from me. Tell her they'll see the tart that she is.'

# Chapter 23

H ope McGrath strode across the moor with teams fanned out alongside. She was walking behind the searchers, watching what they were doing, ready to make a move to any possible find. Joy Grundy was out here somewhere. The woman was probably naked, cold, and maybe even the worst for a beating or whatever else the McDonalds had done to her.

Macleod had remained back at the house and Hope had seen that something was on his mind. He had an obvious concern for Joy Grundy, and Hope knew that's why she was dispatched onto this task. Seoras would be near to useless looking across the moorland. He wasn't as young as a lot of the men who had stepped out now, or as fit as the women that were with her, many volunteers but experts in search. Hope knew the murder team were banking on them.

The teams were not far apart, spread out in a line making their way across the moorland. At times, one would drop down and you couldn't see them due to the topography. Then they'd come back up. So far, Hope felt that they covered the best part of half a mile, and she wondered what the plan was. Should they turn around, search it back? When it came to search and the patterns and methods used, she was quite the novice.

The day was cold, and even though she had a leather jacket on, Hope was feeling it around her knees and around her ears in particular. If she hadn't been working, she'd have untied her hair, let it come down over her ears and keep them warm. She always thought she delivered a more professional look by having her hair tied back up.

She'd spoken briefly to Clarissa, who was making her way out. Ross was handling the procedures back at the station, making sure the McDonalds were successfully locked up awaiting interview. Hope reached a rise in the ground and stood there looking across the long line of searchers before her. Off to the right, some had dropped down, and it was from that gap that she heard a call.

'Here,' somebody cried. 'Here.'

Hope ran over, trailing in behind a search supervisor. She reached the top of a small hillock, clambered down and saw someone pointing at the ground.

'It looks disturbed,' said the woman who had shouted for attention, and the search supervisor stood over it.

'It does, but how fresh is it?'

Hope arrived behind, having heard the conversation. 'I don't care. Let's get a group up here with spades. Start digging.'

The man turned and nodded at Hope but advised that they should continue the search. With Hope's approval, he radioed in, and a number of police officers arrived, complete with shovels to begin digging. Hope told the search advisor to go on with his search and to call her if he found anything else. She remained with the police officers who began to dig.

It was only a few minutes later that the soil broke, and they could see pink skin. Hope reached down and touched the flesh that she saw.

'It's warm,' she said. 'It's warm. Quick, but careful. Dig around. We need to free this woman.'

Of course, she was assuming it was a woman, for all she could see was possibly a hip. Soon, they dug deeper. A buttock was exposed, and then a pair of legs, and Hope advised them to work higher up towards the head. Soon, they saw the shoulders, and digging down with their bare hands, they pulled the woman clear of the soil, turning her over onto her back. She coughed and Hope bent over her, opening up her mouth, but caught the distinct smell of disinfectant.

Hope pulled out her mobile phone, ringing Seoras, urgency in her voice.

'Inspector, we've got her, but there's a smell of disinfectant. It's coming from her mouth.'

'Hang on,' said Macleod, and Hope heard him disappear into the background. He returned some thirty seconds later. 'There's empty bottles of bleach here, it might be the bleach. Get her back quick. I'll get an ambulance here.'

Hope shouted for the search advisor, and soon the entire search line was crowded around them. A coastguard crew arrived with a stretcher and the woman was placed onto it, four blankets placed over her. She was breathing, but her signs were not that great, not surprising as she had ingested a vast quantity of bleach.

'Quick as you can,' said Hope, following the team that were now carrying her across the rough terrain. She marvelled at the speed they were going, considering what they were walking across and how delicately they were carrying the woman. As they got back towards the farmhouse, they could see the ambulance arriving.

Hope veered off when she saw her inspector standing in front of the house. He looked at her up and down.

'You're filthy,' he said, and Hope looked at herself, her hands covered in muck, her jacket soiled, and the jeans she had kneeled down in had large mud stains across them.

'But we got her, Seoras. We've got her.' They watched the ambulance pull away and Macleod went over to the search team that were now sitting on their backsides, puffing heavily after the long carry across the moor.

'Thank you, ladies and gentlemen,' he said. 'You might just have saved her life.' With that, he turned around to the gathered contingent behind him, 'Everyone out on that search, good job. Well done.' He marched over to the search advisor, put out a hand and shook it before turning to Hope. 'We need to be somewhere else.'

'What do you mean?' asked Hope.

'I don't think this is done. I don't think Joy Grundy did anything. Well, nothing against the law anyway. Go get the car, Sergeant.'

Hope looked at her jacket, her Jeans. 'Can I get a minute to wipe my hands?'

'No,' said Macleod. 'Let's go.'

Hope sighed. She marched over to the car, got in, and drove it around to where Macleod stepped in. 'Where to?' asked Hope.

'Annie Spence,' said Macleod.

'You think she's involved in this? I know she was overly keen on you. Are you just looking to ward her off? You don't think she's going to be a target?'

'We need to get to Annie Spence's,' said Macleod. 'Make it

quick, but not so quick I have to hang on.'

Hope smirked at him. 'You're welcome to take the wheel anytime you want, Seoras,' she said as they drove out to the main road.

Arriving at Annie Spence's, they parked in the street and the pair strode to the older woman's house. Macleod ignored the door, going straight to the window with the net curtains.

'She's in there,' he said. 'Like before during the trouble you had, I don't think we'll have any difficulty this time,' and he banged on the window as hard as he could. He saw her come across, bend down and look at him before she turned, walked across the living room and then appeared at the door. It was half open, and she stared at him.

'Macleod, has there been trouble?'

'You could say that.'

'My next-door neighbour said they were arresting people. Is that correct?'

'That is correct,' said Macleod. 'Can I come in?'

'So, you got them then?' she said. 'Macleod got his man. Or was it a woman?'

'I'd like to come in if you don't mind.'

'Make sure she doesn't make a mess of my house.' Macleod turned and looked at Hope, still covered in muck from her search. She stepped inside the front door, took her boots off and her jacket before making her way through. 'She's not coming in those jeans,' said Annie.

'I'm not asking her to come in without them,' said Macleod and walked into the front room.

'Would you like a cup of tea, Inspector?'

Macleod looked at the old woman. There seemed to be more of a life about her this time. 'I'd actually like a coffee,' he said.

'McGrath will have a coffee too. Very kind of you.'

'So, was it Joy Grundy?' asked Annie, walking out of the room. 'Did you find out it was Joy Grundy, Macleod?'

'It wasn't Joy Grundy. Joy Grundy had been kidnapped, but then again, you might have known that.'

'What are you on about, Macleod?' asked Annie as she pressed the kettle.

'Joy Grundy didn't kill anyone. She might be a flirtatious woman, she might be a lonely woman, but she didn't kill anyone. But the McDonalds believed it. Also, Mrs Morgan. Rumours are spread,' he said. 'Funny, isn't it? Funny how you don't have to say much, but the person in the corner hears everything. You can drop in and say, 'I heard this, I heard that,' and they'll believe you because they're never down at the coffee house. Donald MacDonald was. Miranda Folly was. Councillor Morgan was, too. Had you reported on them? Well, you did once this all kicked off. You started speaking to the McDonalds. Not directly, of course. Not the bereaved widow. Oh, no. Somebody went and spoke to the family and the family started talking and somebody whipped it up, "Macleod's not doing anything. Macleod doesn't know. He's been, his detectives been. Look at me, I was attacked."'

'I was attacked, Inspector. I was in the hospital. I got lucky, didn't I?'

'No,' said Macleod as Annie Spence handed him a coffee. 'Shall we go into your dining room?' he said.

'It's a bit formal,' said Annie, 'but if you wish.' She shuffled through and Macleod followed her, placing his cup down on the table. Hope joined him, sitting down, and placing hers in front of her. Annie gulped down her own heartily.

'Quite a range over there of magicians,' said Macleod,

pointing to the display on the wall. 'Where did you learn it?'

'What do you mean?' asked Annie.

'The sleight of hand,' said Macleod. 'That's the way you do it, isn't it? Inconspicuous, sleight of hand. Plenty of other people doing things. Plenty of other things going on. With Donald MacDonald, a sleight of hand to drop in the thallium, then the misdirection, the old biddy coming up to my sergeant. 'Oh, I want Macleod,' like some sort of poor daft sod, all the time diverting the attention away.'

'Why would I do that?' asked Annie. 'What was the point?'

'You really had me,' said Macleod. 'You had me at first until I realised it was about me.'

'What do you mean?'

'You let Sergeant McGrath in, and she saw the pictures. They don't say a lot, but I put together the sleight of hand you might have learnt from your interest in the magicians. After that, it was the interest in me. Constantly, "Macleod, I want Macleod." This whole thing has been about me. You've wanted me near you, giving me a case to solve. You have no real interest in those people. You poisoned three people.'

'And I was poisoned too,' said Annie.

'Clever, that,' said Macleod, 'and leaving the extra on the table for someone to come across. I was impressed with that. The misdirection at first that went to the owners. But then I thought about how it happened. You poisoned someone, Miranda Folly, and everyone turned around and thought it was food poisoning. They actually looked for food poisoning. Well, I don't get out of bed for that. That's not my jurisdiction.

'Then they called for some help, so I sent my sergeant over, because that's not enough for Macleod to take a case. But no, you turned it into more. When Sergeant Urquhart was there, you were surprised it was her. You thought it would be me, so you went and asked. You wanted Macleod. When Sergeant McGrath came round to speak to you, you wanted Macleod. Your obsession was what caught you out. Do you realise that, Annie?'

'It's too late, though,' said Annie. 'Too late.'

'It's not too late. We saved Joy Grundy. You've wrecked a family though. They'll be put up for attempted murder. Joy's in the hospital and I trust they'll save her. Get her stomach pumped, get the bleach out of her, but she'll be all right.'

'It's still too late.'

'Innes will be fine. You were never interested in him. No doubt at some point you'd have stretched it on. If I were still fumbling around in the dark, Joy Grundy would be dead. Next, Innes would follow. You'd even get to Sarah McIver eventually, or would you call it quits, saying Macleod couldn't solve this?'

'But it's too late,' said Annie.

Macleod glanced to his right and saw that Hope had finished half of her cup. 'Put it down,' said Macleod. 'Put it down.'

Hope dropped the cup and it fell off the table, smashing on the wooden floor below. 'Hospital, now,' said Macleod. 'We need to get you to the hospital.'

'What are you on about, sir?' asked Hope.

'She's poisoned you.'

'At last, I get one over Macleod,' said Annie. 'Like I said, it's too late, but it's not her.' Macleod looked over and saw Annie smile. Suddenly, the aged woman seemed to be life and fit. She began doing a little jig. 'This one's beat Macleod,' she said. 'It was hard but I've beat Macleod at last. Oh, you were too good for my little plan, too good for my ruse. Lucky Joy Grundy, eh?

But this time, you know you can't save everyone. You didn't see it, did you?' The woman suddenly clutched her stomach. When Macleod reached forward grabbing her, she began to fall.

'Hope, the car, now.'

Hope took off, grabbing her boots and jacket on the way out while Macleod followed, holding Annie Spence in his arms. He placed her in the backseat, stepped into the front as Hope drove off through the town, screaming along the roads, blasting the horn at anyone in front. When they got to the Western Isles Hospital, Hope got out, carried Annie through, and was directed through to a bed where she placed her down. When they asked what was wrong, Macleod said to them, 'Thallium poisoning, lots of it,' and turned and walked back out to A&E reception. Hope followed him and together, they sat and waited.

# Chapter 24

It had been a long wait and Macleod hadn't left the A&E. When the doctor came out to pronounce that Annie Spence had died, Macleod felt numb. He'd seen through her plot, he'd seen through what she was doing, and yet she had the last laugh. He stood outside the hospital in the car park at three in the morning, feeling the cold on his skin. From behind him, a pair of arms wrapped around his shoulders and pulled him tight.

'It's not your fault, Seoras. She took her own life.'

'I'm not blaming myself,' he said. 'What caused her to do this? What sort of fascination causes this?'

'She had something for you. She felt you were part of her life. She wanted you to be closer. All she wanted was Macleod,' said Hope, 'but then she doesn't know you the way we do.'

'That doesn't help,' said Macleod. 'I'm not finding much humour in this.'

'You saved Joy Grundy,' said Hope. 'They reckon she could be out in a day or two.'

'Yes, we did,' said Macleod, 'but that woman killed three people senselessly. For all that Donald MacDonald was cheating on his wife, I wouldn't have wanted that for him, or for Miranda Folly. Counsellor Morgan, what did he do? Joy Grundy? What was the point of it all, Hope?'

'While you were in waiting, I spoke to Ross. There was a computer at Annie Spence's house. Very simple. Ross said she played solitaire on it most of the time. Her social media had several groups all based on detectives. Most of them were the fictional kind, the ones you see on TV, but she also was in several real crime groups. The thing is, Seoras, she seemed obsessive. She had a post where someone said you could solve everything, get to the bottom of any case, just like those TV detectives, but Annie Spence said no. She said she could best you. Simplest of plots, the simplest of murders.'

'No one flagged this up?'

'Her profile was in a different name, email address that's used for nothing else. She looked the old biddy, but she was anything but. The last entry in the group was posted about half an hour before we got there.'

'She knew. She knew I'd worked it out.'

'She must have done. Guessed you would be coming. Told them you wouldn't get the last piece.'

'She killed herself to prove she could beat me.'

'Exactly,' said Hope. 'You can't deal with that sort of mind. She had a line of small plants in her garden, I saw recently planted. That's where she hid the thallium, under the plants.'

'Come on,' said Macleod. 'It's time to get back to the station. We've got interviews to do, people to arrest and put behind bars.'

'You did what you had to do. Stop blaming yourself.'

'But she stirred the McDonalds up. She stirred up Morgan. Thankfully, that woman had the sense not to get involved, but she poisoned them against Joy Grundy.

CHAPTER 24

'What's the point, Hope? What was the point of it? Who cares? Doesn't she know there's going to be a case I can't solve? I've had plenty of them. They can ask Jane. I went halfway across the world to tell a woman I knew what happened. We never arrested her.'

'She doesn't know that. They all think we got that one right,' said Hope. 'All they saw was a dead body, a man shot dead in a house.'

'Lot to do.' said Macleod. 'Come on.'

\* \* \*

Macleod watched the plate arrive and it was placed in front of Ross who licked his lips. Macleod had never been in a curry house when a sizzling plate arrived. He leaned over, smelling the delicious food that Ross was about to tuck into. His own biryani had arrived, and Macleod took his vegetable curry, pouring it over the rice on his plate. He looked over at Hope who was staring at him, and he simply gave a nod.

She smiled, knowing he was going to be okay. He'd spoken to Jane for an hour or two, talking it through, and as ever, the woman had redirected him, but it was Hope that had encouraged him, told him to talk to her, realised the difficulty that was lying underneath him. He was struggling to come to terms with celebrity, to be somebody that people wanted to challenge.

'Poppadom, Seoras?'

'We've already eaten most of those.'

'There's one left,' said Clarissa. 'Do you want it?'

'Go on then.' Macleod reached over and took the large disk before snapping it and putting it on the side of his plate.

'Do you want a beer with that?' said Sergeant Dolan.

'No, no, never,' said Macleod. 'I don't drink.'

'Well, I'm having one,' said Hope. 'In fact, get a couple of bottles of wine out. This calls for a celebration. We got to the bottom of it, didn't we, sir?'

Macleod looked over at Hope and smiled. 'Seoras. It's Seoras tonight to everyone,' and then he pointed at those from the Stornoway contingent, 'but not a word about it to anyone.'

The table erupted in laughter and Clarissa reached over with a fork, nicking a piece of lamb off Ross' plate. Macleod watched him shout at her as she asked him how he could eat this stuff before looking down at her korma.

The team was good, Macleod decided. It had a hard day with barely any sleep but he knew in the next couple of hours, they'd release the tension. In his head he was still struggling, but he'd be okay.

The McDonalds had been processed, statements had been taken, and they'd go before the court with a charge of attempted murder. In some ways, he felt sorry for them. Of course, he realised just how good Annie Spence was. He'd seen her as the little old lady stuck in the corner, the one who had got lucky when the murderer had tried to poison her, but in retrospect, he felt she was something of a genius, albeit misplaced in where she used her talents.

They'd spoken to her doctor once she'd passed on, and he advised that Annie had no problems with her feet. She didn't need to shuffle, and she'd been in perfect health for years. In fact, he reckoned she could probably run the best part of half a mile, albeit at a comfortable jog at the age of eighty-five. That was impressive, but she'd played them. She'd played everyone.

Ross had looked at her social media group. They were

posting how Macleod had triumphed. He hadn't come and told the Inspector, but Hope had told him afterwards, told him how proud the team was that they'd not been bested, and they knew what a genius was leading them.

Macleod wouldn't have it, and instead, he told them that the curry house up the road from the police station was to be frequented that night. Team celebrations when they got there. It was a long way from where they'd started and they'd certainly not had it on their first case together, but now Hope and he understood each other so much better.

He had looked through the photo album that Annie Spence had collected on him, thought over each of the cases, and begun to appreciate the team that he'd had around him. It was an emotional time, the half-hour he'd spent with it, but as he looked through it, feeling his team's pride, he still couldn't handle this idea of personality, of being some sort of icon.

He told Clarissa and she'd laughed at the word 'icon.' She said more of an antique, whereas Ross had simply said he didn't know why the woman felt like that at all. Good old Ross, simple and direct. Macleod broke apart a piece of naan bread, dipped it in his vegetable curry, placed it in his mouth, laid back, and chewed it thoughtfully. He washed it down with a drink of Coke as he watched Hope pick up a wine glass in one hand and drink freely from it. She was the most unlikely of partners for him, but he had to admire her and not just the way she looked, much more for the way she was. He'd come to know her as a person, as a fine detective. He knew how much she meant to him.

The waiter came over and Hope waved at him shouting for more beer, but the man only smiled at her and instead went around to Macleod.

'Sorry to bother you, Inspector, but there's a woman outside, said she wants to have a word with you.'

'Who?' asked Macleod.

'She didn't say; she just said she wanted to talk to you.'

'Do you want me to get it, Seoras?' asked Hope.

'No,' he said. 'Stay with the team, I'll deal with it. And get them all a round of drinks on me,' he said, to which there was a loud cheer from the table. He got to the end of the table and turned around, 'Non-alcoholic, of course.' There were a few cries, and he was sure that a piece of naan bread hit him in the back, but he didn't care and wandered off to the door of the curry house.

Outside, he saw someone standing in a bright peach jacket. He opened the door and asked did she want to come in, but she said no, and he followed her round the corner, standing in the dark of a streetlight that had gone out.

'I just wanted to apologise,' the woman said to him.

'Miss Grundy, you have nothing to apologise for. You suffered under the most wicked plot and I'm just very glad we got to you before things ran their course.'

'They said that I shouldn't really come out, but I didn't know how long you'd be here for, Inspector. I just wanted to . . .' She stopped, almost struggling with her words.

'It's okay,' said Macleod. 'It was a rough time for everyone.'

'You are right,' she said. 'I think about me a lot. I wanted Donald ahead of Donella. It's not easy when you're on your own.'

'No,' said Macleod, 'it's not.'

'I just didn't want you to have an image of me, a last angry word where I threw you out of the house just because you told me the truth.'

212

'I was harsh with it,' said Macleod, 'I wanted to make sure that you weren't the killer I was looking for.'

'Well, at least that's shown through,' said Joy. 'I'm glad of that.'

Macleod felt the rain begin to fall. It started with a drip and then it began to teem down. Opposite him, Joy Grundy just stood, the rain now soaking her hair.

'Do you think I could actually be with someone for the right reasons?'

'I'm a detective inspector, Miss Grundy. I can suss out how people are, but I'm not a life therapist.'

'Why did she do it? Why did Annie Spence want me to suffer? Did she see me as unworthy? Was I a hypocrite? I know I am. I just don't understand.'

'Annie Spence wasn't after you,' said Macleod, 'she was after me. She had a fascination about me, felt that I wasn't what I was, could best me, could make up a plot so devious I'd never find out.'

'For that, she wanted me to go through this? Inspector, the humiliation I suffered before they put that bleach in my mouth, it was worse, worse than what I suffered in the council chamber when Donald dressed me down. He may have been right on that occasion, but what they did to me . . .'

'I'm truly sorry for that,' said Macleod. 'But listen, you've got a chance to start again. People know you didn't do it and you weren't with Donald. You didn't cheat with him, unlike Miranda. You just struggled, struggled with being lonely.'

'You think I can change?'

'Why not?' said Macleod, suddenly brightening up. 'The weather does.' He looked up at the pouring rain coming down.

'Thank you for my life, Inspector.' Joy Grundy stepped

forward and reached up with a kiss onto Macleod's cheek. 'Tell whoever it is at home that she's a very lucky woman.'

'You don't know me,' said Macleod. 'She has her fair share of troubles.'

'Up and at it tomorrow, is that what you suggest?'

'Yes,' said Macleod, 'up and at it tomorrow, new day and all that. Why don't you get down to the Cortado Club? Show them you don't care. Show them it wasn't you. The things they did to you, you have no reason to be ashamed of them. You've got a lot to offer, Miss Grundy.'

'Will you meet me for coffee in the morning?' she asked.

'Why?' asked Macleod.

'It'll give me a reason to be there. I'm not sure I could walk in if I was just going to be there on my own.'

'I'll be there,' said Macleod, 'and I'll introduce you to someone, a woman called Clarissa. She'll show you how to spit in their face. Right now, I have a large diet Coke awaiting me and a team that needs to celebrate. You're welcome to join us if you want.'

'No, Inspector. That's your people. I can't take that from you.'

'Ten o'clock then,' said Macleod.

'Coffee, and it's on me,' said Joy.

Macleod watched her turn and walk away, the rain still coming down on her hair, her jacket beginning to be soaked. He thought she seemed to carry herself more strongly than before and he hoped so. He had said to Jane, when talking about her, how lovely a woman she was. It was just such a shame. Maybe Clarissa could sort her out. He turned and went back into the curry house and took off his coat. He undid his tie, put it over his seat, and undid the top shirt button.

214

'Are you about to sing?' asked Clarissa.

'You're the only one who would know the songs I sing,' said Macleod, and the table roared with laughter.

'Do it then, Seoras,' she said, putting one arm around him.

'What sort of thing do you old police has-beens sing?' Hope asked.

'*Jailhouse Rock,*' said Clarissa. 'That'll be my era.'

*I'm not that old*, thought Macleod, but he gave a cough, drunk some of his Coke, and assaulted the ears of all before him.

Read on to discover the Patrick Smythe series!

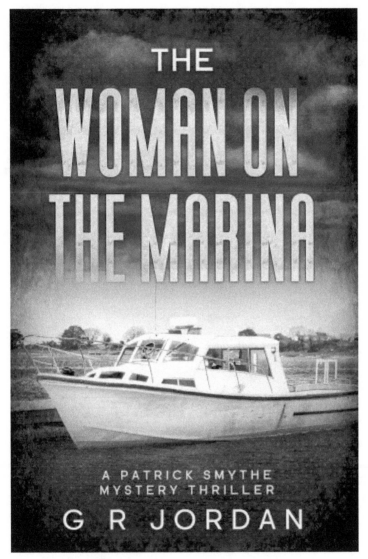

*Start your Patrick Smythe journey here!*

Patrick Smythe is a former Northern Irish policeman who

after suffering an amputation after a bomb blast, takes to the sea between the west coast of Scotland and his homeland to ply his trade as a private investigator. Join Paddy as he tries to work to his own ethics while knowing how to bend the rules he once enforced. Working from his beloved motorboat 'Craigantlet', Paddy decides to rescue a drug mule in this short story from the pen of G R Jordan.

Join G R Jordan's monthly newsletter about forthcoming releases and special writings for his tribe of avid readers and then receive your free Patrick Smythe short story.

Go to https://bit.ly/PatrickSmythe for your Patrick Smythe journey to start!

# About the Author

GR Jordan is a self-published author who finally decided at forty that in order to have an enjoyable lifestyle, his creative beast within would have to be unleashed. His books mirror that conflict in life where acts of decency contend with self-promotion, goodness stares in horror at evil, and kindness blindsides us when we at our worst. Corrupting our world with his parade of wondrous and horrific characters, he highlights everyday tensions with fresh eyes whilst taking his methodical, intelligent mainstays on a roller-coaster ride of dilemmas, all the while suffering the banter of their provocative sidekicks.

A graduate of Loughborough University where he masqueraded as a chemical engineer but ultimately played American football, Gary had worked at changing the shape of cereal flakes and pulled a pallet truck for a living. Watching vegetables freeze at -40'C was another career highlight and he was also one of the Scottish Highlands "blind" air traffic controllers.

These days he has graduated to answering a telephone to people in trouble before telephoning other people to sort it out.

Having flirted with most places in the UK, he is now based in the Isle of Lewis in Scotland where his free time is spent between raising a young family with his wife, writing, figuring out how to work a loom and caring for a small flock of chickens. Luckily, his writing is influenced by his varied work and life experience as the chickens have not been the poetical inspiration he had hoped for!

**You can connect with me on:**
- https://grjordan.com
- https://facebook.com/carpetlessleprechaun

**Subscribe to my newsletter:**
- https://bit.ly/PatrickSmythe

# Also by G R Jordan

G R Jordan writes across multiple genres including crime, dark and action adventure fantasy, feel good fantasy, mystery thriller and horror fantasy. Below is a selection of his work. Whilst all books are available across online stores, signed copies are available at his personal shop.

**Cleared to Die (Highlands & Islands Detective Book 18)**
https://grjordan.com/product/cleared-to-die
**A dead controller killed alone in his tower. A climate of fear and coercion among employees and managers. Can Macleod enter the world of air traffic and bring a safe, orderly, and expeditious solution to the case?**

When a commercial turboprop is forced to go-around on losing communication with Mull tower, the operations team find their oldest controller dead at his post. Amidst a furore over a change of working, Macleod and McGrath find a company in turmoil and with grudges to settle. As the sides are unmasked and the stakes known, can the pair see through the anger and disgruntlement, to bring a brutal killer to justice?

*Silence is golden... unless you need to land!*

**The Hunt for 'Red' Anna (Kirsten Stewart Thrillers #5)**

https://grjordan.com/product/the-hunt-for-red-anna

**London says Anna Hunt is a traitor. Kirsten is dispatched to find and eliminate her boss. Can Kirsten put aside her disbelief to complete her mission or will she find her instincts reveal even stranger truths?**

When Kirsten is called to London, she finds the news of Anna Hunt's defection hard to stomach. With sketchy details, Anna's betrayal seems bizarre and the instruction to eliminate her a brutal response. On hunting down her boss, a plot with an unknown orchestrator gives doubt to every assumption. As the mystery is revealed and secrets laid bare, Kirsten finds her own team under a kill order.

You only ever know someone when you live with them!

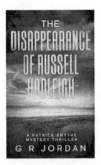

**The Disappearance of Russell Hadleigh (Patrick Smythe Book 1)**
https://grjordan.com/product/the-disappearance-of-russell-hadleigh
**A retired judge fails to meet his golf partner. His wife calls for help while running a fantasy play ring. When Russians start co-opting into a fairly-traded clothing brand, can Paddy untangle the strands before the bodies start littering the golf course?**

In his first full novel, Patrick Smythe, the single-armed former policeman, must infiltrate the golfing social scene to discover the fate of his client's husband. Assisted by a young starlet of the greens, Paddy tries to understand just who bears a grudge and who likes to play in the rough, culminating in a high stakes showdown where lives are hanging by the reaction of a moment. If you love pacey action, suspicious motives and devious characters, then Paddy Smythe operates amongst your kind of people.

Love is a matter of taste but money always demands more of its suitor.

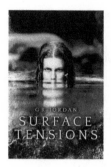

**Surface Tensions (Island Adventures Book 1)**
https://grjordan.com/product/surface-tensions
**Mermaids sighted near a Scottish island. A town exploding in anger and distrust. And Donald's got to get the sexiest fish in town, back in the water.**

"Surface Tensions" is the first story in a series of Island adventures from the pen of G R Jordan. If you love comic moments, cosy adventures and light fantasy action, then you'll love these tales with a twist. Get the book that amazon readers said, "perfectly captures life in the Scottish Hebrides" and that explores "human nature at its best and worst".

Something's stirring the water!

**Corpse Reviver (A Contessa Munroe Mystery #1)**
https://grjordan.com/product/corspe-reviver
**A widowed Contessa flees to the northern waters in search of adventure. An entrepreneur dies on an ice pack excursion. But when the victim starts moonlighting from his locked cabin, can the Contessa uncover the true mystery of his death?**

Catriona Cullodena Munroe, widow of the late Count de Los Palermo, has fled the family home, avoiding the scramble for title and land. As she searches for the life she always wanted, the Contessa, in the company of the autistic and rejected Tiff, must solve the mystery of a man who just won't let his business go.

*Corpse Reviver* is the first murder mystery involving the formidable and sometimes downright rude lady of leisure and her straight talking niece. Bonded by blood, and thrown together by fate, join this pair of thrill seekers as they realise that flirting with danger brings a price to pay.

CPSIA information can be obtained
at www.ICGtesting.com
Printed in the USA
BVHW081812050822
643909BV00002B/121

9 781914 073779